Black Mountain Deception

a novel by

Richard G. Edwards

ISBN 978-0-578-53820-4

Published by EMTCC, LLC, Lexington, Kentucky

Printed in the United States of America on acid-free paper.

The characters and events in this book are fictitious. Any similarity to real persons, living or dead, is coincidental and not intended by the author.

EMTCC, LLC
2019

First Edition

Front Cover
Cover photo by the author is of Black Mountain, Harlan County, Kentucky. Note the radar dome at the top left of the mountain.

Acknowledgements

I would like to sincerely thank Dr. Bill Green, Mr. Jack Sterling, Dr. Gus Peters, and my wife Carolyn for providing many excellent suggestions, comments, and corrections for this novel. Mrs. Kelly Elliott did the expert layout of the book, as well as those for my previous 7 novels. She is truly appreciated!

Pax Tecum!

Dedication

This book is dedicated to my latest grandchild, Eleanor Grace Edwards, who was born on Christmas Eve, 2018. I am super proud of her, and look forward greatly to watching her grow into a young lady!

Preface

This book is my eighth novel. The first five (*Anchor Cross Series*), the sixth (*Nuclear Attack*), the seventh (*The Adventures of Preacher Puss*), and this current novel each have many of the same mountain characters, and are all set in Harlan County, Kentucky. I've tried my best to include a lot of mountain stories and humor reflecting my Kentucky mountain heritage, of which I'm very proud. I've received lots of feedback from those reading my books, and I truly value it. If you have not read my prior novels see their titles listed below. They are all available from Amazon.com and Barnesandnoble.com, or directly from me by just sending a request to my email, as follows:
RICHARDGLENNEDWARDS@GMAIL.COM

I would also greatly value any comments you might care to share with me.

Previous novels by Richard G. Edwards:

1. *Anchor Cross Second Edition*
2. *The Pelle Anchor Cross*
3. *The Helena Anchor Cross*
4. *The Anchor Cross Twins*
5. *The Constantine Anchor Cross*
6. *Nuclear Attack*
7. *The Adventures of Preacher Puss*

Pax Tecum!

Chapter 1

Present Time

October 5

Camp David, Maryland

The four sat around a circular table on the Aspen Lodge patio at Camp David, Maryland. A server brought in a large pitcher of lemonade and sat it in the center of the table along with four glasses. President Thomas DeVore picked up the pitcher and poured each glass full. He then sat back in his chair with his glass in hand, a smile on his face, and looked at each of the other three men and said, "Gentlemen, I know it was inconvenient for you to be here today. It's Saturday, and we should each be with our families on this glorious fall day. But we have some extremely important business to discuss, and I appreciate so much your adjusting your schedules to accommodate me." He then held his lemonade glass out at arm's length, and all four clanked their glasses together. "So, let me begin."

President DeVore looked directly at Rudy Lester, Director of the Central Intelligence Agency, and said, "Rudy here has passed some very disturbing information to me. A mole we have in North Korea has informed us that a very sophisticated operation is well underway to launch a nuclear bomb from our soil. This bomb will be launched by a sub-orbital rocket that will take it to a sufficiently high altitude and then detonate. The resulting nuclear explosion will be large enough to produce an electromagnetic pulse capable of destroying most of our electronics, including those that operate automobiles, airplanes, power plants, computers, etc.

I think you get the idea. If this happens, our country could well be brought to a standstill. Many people would die, and we could be extremely vulnerable to attack."

"Did I describe it properly, Rudy?"

Director Lester replied, "Unfortunately, yes you did Mr. President. The resulting pulse is called a high-altitude electromagnetic pulse, or HEMP. We conducted a test of this type in July, 1962 above the mid-Pacific ocean, and it demonstrated that the effects were much larger than had been previously calculated. The test was called Starfish

Prime, and its effects became public when it knocked out streetlights, burglar alarms, and microwave links in Hawaii, about 900 miles away from the detonation point."

Secretary of Defense Sam Back and Secretary of Homeland Security Josh Dillon each got very worried looks on their faces. President DeVore nodded affirmatively.

The President then said, "Yeah, that's right. We've got a major problem facing us."

"How accurate is this intelligence?" asked Secretary Back. "Do we know it is credible?"

"We think there's at least a 95% chance it's accurate," replied Director Lester. "In addition to our mole, we've gotten supporting information from other reliable sources. Also, the internet has been popping with lots of curious messages that relate to a major upcoming event labeled Project Bee Sting. We don't understand yet the significance of the term Bee Sting, but the messages seem to indicate a major hit on U.S. soil around Thanksgiving."

Josh Dillon said, "That's only a little less than 8 weeks from now! Is there any indication where this might take place?"

Director Lester replied, "From the information we've been able to put together, we think there is a high probability that the launch will be from Kentucky. As each of you know, Kim Jong-un has attempted several unsuccessful attacks in Harlan County, Kentucky, and our sources tell us that he would likely pick a site there in retaliation. Also, there are lots of very remote areas there that could possibly hide the launch site."

"Hard to imagine," replied the President. "To successfully launch a sub-orbital rocket an awfully lot of land would have to be disturbed. Surely that activity could be readily noticed or picked up by satellite."

"You'd think so," said Rudy Lester, "but we think they've been at this operation for about a year and have likely put together some kind of cover for the launch site. What I mean is they likely have taken over an existing business somewhere or started one of their own that looks legit but is actually nothing but cover for the launch."

"Where did the damn rocket come from?," asked President DeVore, "and the nuclear warhead? Do we know information on the size of the rocket? And do we know for sure that they've already been delivered to Harlan County?"

"Good questions, Mr. President," said Rudy Lester. "Our mole in North Korea was not able to find out any specifics about where the rocket and warhead came from. They could be North Korean, Russian, Iranian, or even American....we just don't know. The mole was able to only get the size information....3000 pounds, 40 feet high and

2 feet in diameter. And yes, our sources definitely think both the rocket and the warhead are currently in place.... somewhere in Harlan County."

"I still question why Chairman Kim would select Kentucky just for retaliation. Would a launch from Kentucky accomplish the desired effect he would want?" asked Sam Back.

"It would," said Rudy Lester. "It would create severe consequences for all of the Eastern U.S. Everything East of the Mississippi River. It'd get all our East Coast, including Washington, New York and Boston."

The President then said, "So, gentlemen, as I said before, it looks like we've got ourselves a real problem! Director Lester just put this all together a few days ago. Our next step is to send agents to Harlan County to solicit their assistance. Obviously, we'll have to keep under wrap the true mission, but I think the agents can talk in general to law enforcement in the county and try and get their help in locating this launch operation."

All four men then took long sips of their lemonade, and then all nodded in agreement.

Secretary of Defense Back said, "God speed, and Lord help us if they're not successful!

Chapter 2

One Year Earlier
Pyongyang, North Korea

Chairman Kim Jong-un sat at his desk in his Pyongyang palace. General Ri Kwang-choi stood at attention before him. Kim was just finishing a mid-morning snack of two cheesburgers and a chocolate milkshake. When finished he wiped his mouth with a napkin and then looked directly at General Ri and said, "Ri, what you have discovered is of tremendous interest to me. Let me tell you what I understand from your report. First of all, there is a person that currently resides in the state of Virginia in the United States that has possession of a rocket, called an Aerobee 170A, that is in good working order and is capable of launching a payload of approximately 500 pounds to an altitude of approximately 120 miles. Secondly, this person would be willing to work with us. Is that correct?"

General Ri replied, "That is correct, Chairman Kim. The person lives in the Virginia town of Chincoteague, located on a small island off the Atlantic coast. His name is Ralph Keelen, but he has the nickname "Geek". He is called Geek Keelen, and is called this because he is a genius with the computer. My understanding is that he is a bit strange, and has very few friends. He lives on a farm that was owned by his parents. They both died, and he inherited the farm. Geek Keelen works for the nearby Wallops Island Flight Facility. This facility was founded in 1945 for Naval Aircraft, but in more recent years has become a launch facility for NASA rockets. Geek Keelen's father worked at Wallops Island also, and for a hobby he was active as a pilot of glider airplanes. Several others working at Wallops Island had a similar interest, and the group formed a club for flying the gliders from Wallops. It was ideal because the base was previously developed for aircraft, but no longer used for that purpose. The glider club grew to have about 75 members, and the government gave them a building on the base to house their gliders. That building was quite large, and the club developed a part of it into a museum for glider aircraft. When the facility started launching small rockets for NASA, the glider museum started to acquire obsolete rockets in addition to the gliders. One of the prize gifts from NASA to the museum was an Aerobee 170A rocket. NASA gave them this rocket when they retired it in 1985. After Geek Keelen's father died, Geek became active in the museum. In 2015 NASA decided it needed the land where the museum building stood, and told the Club that they had to move the museum. The club had little money and nowhere to move the museum. Geek volunteered to take all the museum rockets and store them in a large barn on his farm. He did, and therefore currently has the Aerobee stored there and in perfect working condition. One of our assets also works at Wallops Island and knows Geek Keelen. He said he was almost sure that for enough money he would sell the rocket and also work to help launch it."

"I see," Chairman Kim replied. "If this is true, then I have a plan that would require his cooperation. Do you feel our person could recruit him and the rocket if offered 5 million U.S. dollars?"

General Ri's chin dropped, and then he said, "For that amount of money I think we could own him and the Aerobee."

"Then let me explain my plan to you, General Ri. We buy Geek Keelen and his Aerobee and make arrangements to transport both of them to Kentucky. I have had extensive discussions with Dr. Pak Yong-ho, head of our nuclear development program. He has assured me that we currently have a nuclear bomb that weighs under 500 pounds and is of a size that could be incorporated into the payload of the Aerobee 170A. He also assures me that this nuclear bomb, when exploded at an altitude of 120 miles above Kentucky would produce an electromagnetic pulse that would cripple everything electronic east of the U.S. Mississippi River. This would result in massive American deaths and would bring the U.S. to their knees. We could then make demands of them with the threat that we would detonate another similar bomb over the Western U.S. if our demands were not met. We would own them."

General Ri's eyes got large and seemed to glow as he said, "Mr. Chairman, that plan sounds very doable. Much work would need to be done in recruiting Mr. Keelen and the Aerobee, and then getting them both to Kentucky without being discovered. And then we would have to work out a plan to get the bomb there as well. But I'm sure that could all be arranged. With your permission, I can get started on it immediately."

Chairman Kim nodded his head slowly and then said, "Get on it. Lets plan to meet weekly until we have all the arrangements made. I would like to execute my plan, which I have nicknamed Bee Sting, during the American Thanksgiving holiday next year. Their Thanksgiving is the busiest time of the year for travel, and that would result in the maximum number of deaths from our bomb. Fourteen months should give us time to make sure everything is set up and ready to go. The Aerobee will indeed deliver a big sting!"

Chairman Kim stood and walked around his desk to General Ri. The two shook hands and then the Chairman patted Ri on his back as he turned and left the Chairman's office.

Chapter 3

Present Time

October 8

Harlan, Kentucky

The Harlan County Court House is located in the center of town in Harlan. Offices for the Harlan County Sheriff are located in the court house. Directly across the street, Central Street, from the court house is Creech Cafe, owned by the Mayor of Harlan, Fred Knapp, and a very popular hang-out for both school kids and adults.

Mayor Knapp was standing at the cash register in his store sipping coffee as he noticed the large, black Suburban with government license plates pull into a loading zone in front of his store. He continued to watch as two men emerged from it, both wearing dark suits with ties. Each carried a brief case. After looking around they crossed the street and headed for the court house.

Deputy Sheriff Rosie Cain spent 90% of her time in the Sheriff's Department doing routine clerical jobs, answering the phone, assisting anyone coming into the office, and doing anything else that Sheriff J. Bert Sterling asked of her. The sheriff's office was small, consisting of the entrance room with a counter behind which Rosie worked, a deputy desk in one corner of the room for the sheriff's principal deputy, Kyle Potter, an office for the sheriff located through a door behind the counter, a six person holding cell located behind the sheriff's office, a small storage room, and a bathroom. One other very unique feature of the office was a small plywood shelf that had been added to the wall beside the entrance door and above Deputy Potter's desk. On this shelf resided Preacher Puss, the Harlan County Sheriff's Department's mascot. She is a 15 pound grey tabby cat that had been adopted by Rosie when at a very young age she was trapped in the back of a small county church that caught on fire. The firemen rescued her when they heard her screaming at the top of her lungs. They took her to the sheriff's office when no one else claimed her, and when they related her story to Rosie she immediately named her Preacher Puss, since she was found screaming in a church. The cat loved living in the sheriff's department, and had acquired quite a reputation for subduing crooks. As it turns out, she had acquired an intense hatred for guns when at a young age she had wittnesed two other cats get shot by a very mean man. Since that, anytime she saw someone with a gun in their hand she would do anything in her power to make them release it. Usually this meant jumping onto the person's hand and/or arm with her claws extended and digging in. She had subdued several crooks that way, and had played an important part in the capture of many other bad guys. Her reputation had grown throughout the law enforcement and local communities. She had even been made an honorary Deputy Sheriff. She spent most of her time napping on the shelf above the entrance door. She would occasionally open one eye to see what was going on, and gently swish her tail back and forth. Most people that entered the office would greet her and reach up and give her a pet. She would usually reply with a gentle meow. Preacher Puss was a very unusual and special cat.

Rosie had just completed a phone call when the front door opened and two men dressed in dark suits and ties entered. Rosie said, "Good morning guys....what can I do for you?"

Both men immediately reached into the breast pocket of their suit coats and pulled out leather identification wallets. They each flipped them open, showing a badge, their photo, and affiliation information.

Dark suit #1 said, "Good morning deputy. My name is Cody Short. I'm an agent with the CIA."

Dark suit #2 said, "And I'm Special Agent Sammy King with the FBI."

Rosie's mouth dropped open. Then she said, "I'm very pleased to meet you. I'm Deputy Sheriff Rosie Cain. We seldom get G-men here in our office. We're honored. What can I do for you?"

"We would like to talk with Sheriff Sterling," replied Agent Short. "Is he in?"

"He is," said Rosie. "Please just have a seat and I'll let him know you're here."

The two nodded in agreement and sat in chairs against the wall.

Rosie knocked on the door to the sheriff's office and then walked in, shutting the door behind her.

Sheriff Sterling said, "Well, Rosie, please do come in! Your face looks flushed. I'll bet you have some news for me."

Rosie grinned and said, "Boy....do I! We've got two G-men sitting out there in my office! One's from the CIA and the other is an FBI agent. They said they want to talk with you."

Bert laughed and said, "I must admit that's a little unusual for us! How about I go out and meet them!"

Bert stood from his desk and walked around in front and joined Rosie going back into the entrance office.

The two G-men stood. Bert shook hands with each of them as they introduced themselves. Bert then said, "Please, do come into my office. I have coffee made. Could I get you a cup."

Each man nodded in agreement as they entered Bert's office and took a seat.

Bert poured each a cup of coffee and, after walking back around his desk and taking a seat said, "Two G-men in dark suits in Harlan are a bit unusual. I sure hope the Sheriff's Department hasn't done anything wrong!"

Without smiling Cody Short said, "No, our business has nothing to do with anything amiss in your department, sheriff. As a matter of fact, everything we've learned about your operation is very, very positive. You seem to run a good ship."

"Thanks," Bert replied. "We try. So what brings you to Harlan?"

"A very important and urgent matter," Sammy King said. "Let me say at the outset that there are certain aspects of the situation which we're about to discuss with you that we cannot share. I'm sure you understand."

"I'll try," the sheriff replied with a smile.

Agent Short then said, "The situation we're here about regards national security. We think there is a highly credible threat present somewhere here in Harlan County. Our job is to secure your assistance to help us find this threat and eliminate it."

Bert said, "I see. Well, this sounds very, very serious. Certainly my office stands ready to assist anyway we can. But we're going to have to know a little more to be able to help."

"Of course," said Cody Short. "Here's what I can tell you. The threat involves the firing of a rocket from somewhere in the county. The rocket is about 40 feet long, 2 feet wide, and weighs 3,000 pounds. It is of the type that is fired from the ground in a upright position. We have reason to believe that the rocket likely is currently located somewhere in your county. Furthermore, it could well already have been here for some period of time, possibly for a year or more. We think that the bad guys have either purchased an existing piece of property or business, or maybe have bought or leased land and built a suitable structure to house and fire the rocket. Starting tomorrow we'll have helicopters running a grid pattern over the county to see if they can spot anything suspicious. We would like your assistance to have your deputies on the lookout, and we would like to have help in searching the court records for activity over the past year regarding new land purchases, leases, rentals, etc. Any records that could point to an activity that could accommodate the rocket. I know it's a tall order, but I can't impress on you how extremely important and time sensitive it is."

The sheriff looked at each of the men for a moment and then said, "Gentlemen, my office has a total of 11 employees. Six of those are here in Harlan, and five are located in a satellite office in Cumberland, about 25 miles Northeast of Harlan on highway 119. Harlan County is pretty large, area wise. We have 468 square miles. I don't know how much time we're talking about here, but given the size of the county and the limited manpower I'd say we're going to have to come up with a plan that maximizes the probability of a find within the time we have. Any ideas?"

"You bet we do," Agent Short replied. "We've had numerous meetings and many people thinking about various possibilities. One idea was to use the National Guard to comb the entire county, but it was decided that that action would cause far too much disturbance, and once begun would undoubtedly alert the bad guys that they were being hunted in that manner. We still could utilize them, but for the time being they remain only a contingency action. We also considered publicizing the search using television, radio, and newspapers. If we did this, it would only be effective if someone immediately recognized the bad guys and came forth with the information. Otherwise, it too would alert them to our search. And other ways were discussed as well, but what we decided would work best would be a systematic search of the county utilizing your deputies. We knew the size of your force, and thought if you would agree we could divide up the county into grids of about 40 square miles each and have one of your deputies responsible for searching each grid. We liked this option because your deputies are familiar with the area and the people, and we think this action would most likely be the best route to take. We're aware that you and your deputies have your regular duties to attend to as well, and that the search would have to be done in conjunction with those. Also, we were hoping that Deputy Cain could run the records search here in the court house for us. If this would be agreeable with you, that would leave yourself, 9 deputies, and Agent King and myself, a total of 12, to search the county. Since Sammy and I are not familiar with the area or the people, we thought that perhaps we could search along major roadways. What do you think?"

Sheriff Sterling thought for a moment, and then said, "Well, I think I understand what you would like to do. But you still haven't given me a time frame. How long would we have to accomplish the search?"

Agent King jumped in, "The current information we have is that the rocket would likely be fired sometime during the Thanksgiving holiday period. This year Thanksgiving is on November 28th. So we think sometime starting on Wednesday November 27th to Sunday evening December 1st. Since today is October 8th, we have just about 7 weeks."

"It is a tall order," Sheriff Sterling replied. "And we'd need to have some cock-and-bull story to feed to the people. We couldn't very well tell them we were searching for a 3000 pound rocket. Everyone in Harlan County would leave immediately if that word got out!"

"You are exactly correct, sheriff," Agent Short said. "What we thought would work would be to tell them that the sheriff's office is searching for a large shipment of drugs that had gotten into the county and hidden. That way it would look perfectly normal for the deputies to ask to look throughout homes and businesses, as well as to be searching remote areas. We even thought that a news release could go out from your department to the media alerting them of the search. When the bad guys saw or heard this news it wouldn't tip them off. What are your thoughts?"

"I like it," Bert said. "We could always say to any business or home owner that we were not suspicious of them, but that we had reason to believe that the drugs might be stored in a location unknown to the owner. In other words, that they were secretly stored. In private homes that could mean in basements or remote buildings. I think we could make that work."

"I don't mean to offend you in any way with what I'm about to say, Sheriff Sterling," Agent King then said, "but how trustworthy do you think your deputies would be to keep the whole rocket thing under wraps? We obviously would need to tell them what they were searching for, and we all know that people like to talk. If the fact got out that a 3000 pound rocket was the real reason for the search, word would spread like wildfire. What are your thoughts here?"

Bert nodded in agreement, and said, "I know exactly what you're asking. All of my deputies have great track records. We don't have any new recruits. The youngest deputy we have has been on the force for almost 5 years. But you are right.....people do like to talk. I think the best approach would be to have a staff meeting, one here in Harlan and another in Cumberland for the satellite office, to tell all the deputies the cover story and then have the two of you along with myself describe the importance of keeping the whole rocket thing under wraps. Not even a word to family members or close friends. I think it'll boil down to just having to trust them. The appearance of you two G-men will go a long way to achieving that goal. Given the time constraints, I would suggest the staff meetings be set up for tomorrow afternoon. We can start here at 1pm, and then drive to Cumberland and have that meeting at 3:30 pm. Would that be agreeable?"

The two agents nodded in agreement. Agent King said, "That sounds fine. And we could inform Deputy Cain of her duties at the meeting here tomorrow. Also, I think we should schedule weekly progress meetings, and agree on a procedure for reporting anything suspicious."

The sheriff responded, "Yes, and why don't we plan to have the meetings both here and in Cumberland, on Friday's starting at 1 and 3:30 pm, respectively."

The two agents stood and extended their hands across the desk to Sheriff Sterling. They shook hands and the sheriff lead the way out of his office.

As the three men entered the entrance office Deputy Cain said, "Well gentlemen, I trust the meeting went well."

Bert replied, "It did indeed, Rosie. Please schedule a staff meeting for all deputies for tomorrow. Here in Harlan for 1 pm, and in Cumberland for 3:30 pm."

"Will do, chief," replied. Rosie.

Bert walked back into his office and closed the door behind him. The two G-men began walking toward the door to exit when Agent Short noticed Preacher Puss lying on her shelf bed above Deputy Potter's desk and beside the door. Agent Short said, "Deputy Cain, that sure is a good looking cat there. Is it a mascot?"

Rosie said, "She sure is. Her name is Preacher Puss, and she's a very, very special cat."

Agent King then said as Agent Short reached up and stroked Preacher Puss, "Oh, what's so special about her?

"She has quite a reputation for subduing crooks, Agent King."

Agent Short then pulled his hand down from Preacher Puss, looked at Rosie, and said, "Surely you're kidding. She's just a cat! How could she possibly do anything to subdue a crook?"

Rosie replied, "Well, let me just say she has a thing about not liking to see guns."

With that, Agent Short reached inside his coat and withdrew a pistol. He cocked it, extended it out, and said, "Oh, you mean guns like this?"

A huge mistake. Rosie's face immediately turned pale, and then all heard a noise that sounded like a combination scream and rushing wind. Preacher Puss landed atop

Agent Short's outstretched hand and arm. Her claws were extended and dug deeply into the agent."

The cry of pain from the CIA Agent was so sharp and loud that Sheriff Sterling came rushing from his office. He shouted, "What's going on?"

Blood was gushing down the arm and hand of Agent Short. Preacher Puss clung on. The agent dropped the gun to the floor, at which time two things happened simultaneously. Preacher Puss immediately released Agent Short and jumped back to her shelf, curled up, and closed her eyes. The pistol fell to the floor and went off, firing a bullet up and just outside the back of Agent King's left leg. It then passed under the back of his jacket, through the left cheek of his rear end, then out the top of his jacket and lodged into the ceiling.

Agent King screamed, grabbed his rear and yelled, "I've been shot!"

Blood then started to appear at Agent King's feet.

Rosie ran quickly and grabbed the office emergency first-aid kit, and she and Bert ran to the two agents. Rosie said, "Bert, I'll take care of Agent Short, you take Agent King into the bathroom and check him out."

Bert and Sammy King rushed to the bathroom. Rosie removed antiseptic, gauze, and bandage and began cleaning Cody Short's wounds.

Shortly, the sheriff and Agent King returned to the entrance office.

Bert said, "Rosie, I'm going to take these two gentlemen to the hospital. They may need some shots, and better wound dressings. I'll be back as soon as possible. Call if you need me."

"You bet, will do," replied Rosie. "Good luck guys."

The two agents mumbled something under their breath, and both looked sourly at Preacher Puss as they went out the door. After the door was closed Rosie walked over close to Preacher Puss's shelf. The cat stood up and looked at Rosie with her head cocked to one side. Rosie reached out and held her right palm inches away from the cat. Preacher Puss then raised her right paw and swiped it through Rosie's right palm. Rosie laughed loudly and said, "Preacher Puss, for someone from our country's highest intelligence agency, that Agent Short sure didn't show any signs of intelligence when he drew his gun. I guess they'll believe my story now about how you dislike guns."

Rosie reached up and stroked Preacher Puss several times, and then reached in her pocket and pulled out three Whisker Lickin cat treats for her. As she laid the treats on the shelf Preacher Puss purred loudly, swished her tail several times, and proceeded to woof down the treats. She then laid back down, closed her eyes, and continued with her nap.

Rosie said, "Preacher Puss, it may be a while before this story gets out, but when it does I'm sure Harlan will talk and joke about it for a long time. Deputy Preacher Puss attacks one G-man and causes another to get shot in the derriere.....only they'll more likely use another word, one with three letters that begins with 'a'."

· · ·

Sheriff Sterling and the two G-men climbed into the sheriff's cruiser and started driving toward the Appalachian Regional Hospital, only about 3 miles from downtown Harlan. As they drove, the sheriff said, "Guys, I'm really sorry about this. Preacher Puss just cannot stand to see a gun drawn. I hope you understand."

Agent Short said, "No problem sheriff. It was totally my fault. I don't know what got into me that caused me to draw my weapon. It was only intended as a joke, but it sure was taken seriously by that cat. And, of course, Sammy getting shot was totally my fault as well. If I had not drawn my gun it wouldn't have happened. I do understand now what Deputy Cain meant when she said the cat was very, very special. Preacher Puss will have my full respect in the future."

Agent King nodded with a smile on his face and said, "I'll ditto that. I may have a sore butt for a while, but I'm just really lucky the bullet went through without doing any damage. I'll be fine in a day or two. Let's just forget the incident."

"Great," Bert replied. "I did have one more thought I wanted to share with you about the upcoming investigation....and how about if we refer to it our Project 'BS'. The locals will all take that to mean something different, but we'll know it refers to Project Bee Sting, what ever that means. The thought I wanted to share was that we have a truly outstanding Mayor in Harlan. His name is Fred Knapp, and he owns and operates Creech Cafe, directly across the street from the court house."

"Yeah," answered Cody Short. "We parked our Suburban in a loading zone in front of it." Didn't know the mayor owned it. Hope he won't be mad at us."

Bert laughed, "I think it'll be okay. Anyway, Fred is extremely knowledgeable about everything that goes on in the county. He's been around for many years, and is one of the most intelligent, friendly, and reliable people I know. I would like for him to be aware of our Project BS. He'll certainly agree to not divulge the rocket information, and I think he might well be extremely valuable to our effort."

Agent King looked at Agent Short. They both nodded in agreement, and Cody Short said, "We need all the good help we can get. I think that's an excellent idea."

"Super. When I take you back to your Suburban after our hospital visit maybe we could stop in Creech Cafe for a brief visit with the mayor. I'll introduce you guys, if that's okay."

Both agents nodded in agreement. Bert pulled into the hospital parking lot.

• • •

2 hours later

Fred Knapp was sitting at a back table in his cafe sipping coffee. He heard the doorbell tinkle and looked up to see the sheriff walk in with two suits behind him. It was about 2 pm, and school was not yet out for the day, and there were only a few other customers sitting around the cafe chatting and having snacks. Two unusual features were apparent to any entering Creech Cafe. The first was a large green parrot, named Polly, that sat on a perch most of the time near the cash register. Fred had had Polly for many years, and all who frequented the restaurant were aware of her presence. She usually mooched for food, and had quite a vocabulary. She recognized many of the locals when they came in, and called them by name. If her mooching was unsuccessful, she could be known to let loose with a long tirade of not so pleasant words. Most people fed her. The other unusual feature of the cafe is the walls. They are all plastered with photographs, newspaper articles, magazine articles, and anything else that Fred declared worthy to grace his walls. Fred loved to chat with the customers about any of these. He could spend hours relating stories about the wall-coverings. And all the customers loved to hear them. In addition, Fred knew all the latest jokes, and was always ready to share them as well. The people in Harlan and Harlan County loved Fred. No wonder he was mayor.

Fred stood, threw up his arms, and yelled, "Hey sheriff....you guys come back here and join me." The three men walked back to Fred's table, and Bert made the introductions and briefly explained the encounter with Preacher Puss as the cause of Agent Long's bandages on his right arm and hand and the fact that Agent King was carrying a small cushion. Fred grinned as he noticed the dark stains on their suits and as Agent King sat gingerly on his cushion. He said, "Okay, you are the two with the black Suburban parked in my loading zone out there."

"Sorry Mr. Mayor,' said Agent King. It was handy when we got here, but we certainly didn't know it belonged to the mayor. I hope it's not caused you any problem."

"Not at all," Fred replied. "Haven't had any deliveries since you parked. I happened to notice you when you got here, and when I saw the government tags I certainly wasn't going to cause a problem," Fred said with a grin.

Bert said, "Fred, I wanted you to meet these guys, and I'm getting ready to tell you the reason they're here. I told them you are one super mayor, and that your help could well be very valuable to them. Of course they want what I'm getting ready to tell you to remain strictly confidential."

Fred agreed, and Bert related to him what the two agents had told him. No one was sitting close to the mayor's table. After he heard the story he looked at Bert and quietly said, "My word......a 3000 pound rocket in Harlan County? It's a good thing you came up with the drugs cock-and-bull story. If word got out about that rocket I think we'd likely see an exodus. That is really scary. I'll certainly be glad to do anything I can to help with Project BS. I really like that name!!"

"Thanks Fred," Bert replied. "Maybe you could join us for our staff meeting tomorrow at 1 pm in my office. We're going to kick off Project BS."

"I'll be there," the mayor replied. All then stood and shook hands, and were getting ready to leave when Bert said, "Mayor, how about one of your stories to send us happily on our way?"

Fred thought a moment and then replied. "Absolutely. Heard a good one this morning. This couple was having a party celebrating their 50th wedding anniversary, and one of the attendees asked the husband what was the key to their long marriage. The husband replied, "Well, just before we got married we talked about how things would be. I popped up and said, 'Honey, when there are any major decisions to be made during our marriage I'll make em. You can make all the other decisions.' And you know what, we haven't had to make a single major decision since we got married!"

Bert and the two agents roared with laughter as they left Creech Cafe. All three patted Fred on the back. Polly said, "Come back gentlemen!". The G-men got in their black Suburban and drove away. Bert walked across the street to his office with a smile on his face .

Chapter 4

8 Months Earlier
Chincoteague, Virginia

Mr. Lee Kon sat at the bar in the Pony Pines restaurant. It was Tuesday, and he had just gotten off work at Wallops Island. Lee worked for NASA as an electrician. He was anticipating a meeting with his friend.

• • •

Lee Kon was 40 years old. He had been born in a small town in east central North Korea. The government had identified him at an early age as an unusually intelligent person and had enrolled him in a special school. He had 9 others in his class at the school. All had been selected because of their high intelligence. They had been trained in different disciplines, but all had received extensive foreign language classes as well as those in North Korean and world history, plus the usual reading, writing, and arithmetic. Lee had been trained as an electrician, and had excelled in the English language. Upon completion of the program, usually around the age of 25, each member of the class was assigned to a job in North Korea until a suitable foreign assignment was found. Lee was married when he was 27, and now had two children, both boys. When he turned 30 he received an order from his government that he was to travel to the United States and there become a citizen. Paperwork had been processed that listed him as a North Korean seeking asylum in the U.S. He was told that he would establish residence in Chincoteague, Virginia and apply for a job at the NASA base at nearby Wallops Island. In addition to the salary he would receive as an electrician, the North Korean government would pay him a monthly stipend and would fly him back home for family visits twice a year. He had also received $10,000 initially to get him relocated. He rented an apartment in Chincoteague, and after about 6 months got the job at Wallops Island. He was a mole for the North Korean government, and reported to them weekly via a special satellite phone. He reported everything he learned that was going on at the NASA base, and on occasion was given special assignments to do certain jobs. About a month after he began work at Wallops Island he visited the glider and rocket museum there and met Geek Keelen. They became friends, and began to socialize after work....usually by meeting at the Pony Pines restaurant for meals and drinks. During one of these meetings Geek confided to Lee that the museum was to be closed and that he had volunteered to store the rockets in a barn on his property until another location could be secured. And during this conversation he told Lee about the prize Aerobee 170A. Lee was already familiar with the rocket, having carefully observed it in the museum. He then reported this to North Korea, and from this information Project Bee Sting was put together.

•   •   •

Lee felt a slap on his back and turned from the bar to see his friend Geek Keelen. Lee said, "Hey, my friend, we meet again! I have something special I want to talk to you about in private. How about we grab a booth, have a few drinks and a meal, and then I'll tell you what I've got in mind?"

"Sure Lee, sounds good to me. I see one over there in the corner that looks isolated. That one okay?"

"Absolutely," Lee replied as the two men walked to the booth and sat.

After a couple of drinks, small talk, and a delicious meal of Chincoteague oysters Geek sat back in the booth and said, "Another super meal. The oysters here are absolutely the greatest. Now Lee, tell me what you have in mind."

Lee began, "Geek, I think we are good friends and know each other pretty well. You know that I'm a native of North Korea, and came to the U.S. seeking political asylum. As it turns out I do still have connections in North Korea, and I was recently contacted by one of these asking if I would assist in setting up an operation that would result in bringing new respect for North Korea. Kim Jong-un does not think that the U.S. has the proper respect for his country, and he would like to change that. If there was enough compensation available to you do you think you might be interested in helping me?"

Geek looked directly at Lee, and after several seconds said, "I don't think I know what you're asking of me. Would I be interested in making some extra money? Sure. But I don't think I would want to do anything to betray my country, if that was a part of it."

"No, no....nothing like that," Lee replied. "You wouldn't be betraying your country, you would just be helping North Korea to gain respect."

"Well, I'd have to think about it," Geek said. "What about the compensation part, and what exactly would I have to do?"

"How does 5 million dollars sound?"

"You've got to be kidding," Geek said. "How could I possibly be worth that kind of money to North Korea?"

"You are," replied Lee. "You are extremely fortunate to be in the position you are in."

"And what might that be?" asked Geek.

"You have that Aerobee 170A stored at your farm. And you have the knowledge of how to operate it. My country would like to fire it from American soil as a demonstration of its power. A warhead would be placed on the rocket, but it would only be detonated at its maximum altitude, about 120 miles up. It would produce an electromagnetic pulse that would cause problems for anything electronic, but would not destroy people like the bombs dropped on Japan at the end of World War II. It would simply be a demonstration that Kim Jong-un has the power to cause problems for the U.S. This would bring him the respect he seeks. For that, he's willing to pay you 5 million dollars."

"Wow. Double Wow!!" said Geek. "That certainly is a lot of dough. I'll have to think about this, and we'll get back together to talk particulars if I decide I want to do it. Is that okay?

"Sure," replied Lee. "You think about it. If you decide you want to help then we'll discuss all the particulars. And think about what you could do with 5 million dollars!"

Chapter 5

Present Time

October 9

Harlan, Kentucky

Sheriff Sterling sat behind his desk and looked at the gathering in his office. His chief deputy Kyle Potter sat to the extreme left, and then Deputies Simpson Brown, Mousy Giles, and Bill Black all in a row beside Deputy Potter. Deputy Rosie Cain had a chair in the extreme back next to the door in case someone came into the office or she needed to take a phone call. Beside Sheriff Sterling on his right sat Mayor Fred Knapp, and on the sheriff's left Agents Short and King were seated. Each person had been introduced as they entered the room.

Bert looked at his watch and said, "Folks, it's 1 o'clock. Time to get started." He then proceeded to tell his deputies the Project BS particulars and then the drug story that was to be used while searching the county. He produced and distributed maps that contained a grid of about 40 square miles of Harlan County to each of the deputies. Each grid was different and was assigned to a particular deputy. He explained Deputy Rosie Cain's task to go through all the pertinent Court House records to look for suspicious new businesses and/or building projects in the county over the past couple of years. He then explained the time limitation they had in their search, and that the search had to be carried out in conjunction with their regular duties.

Bert then looked at the two G-men sitting on his left and said, "These two fellows, Agents Short and King, have agreed to help in any way possible. They each have a grid along major highways in the county, and will be searching homes and businesses along these. I think they may have a word they would like to share with you. Agent Short."

Cody Short said, "Thanks Sheriff, and I certainly want to thank you for jumping right on this project, and for arranging for the assistance of your deputies. Let me just say it as plainly as I can, the national security of the United States depends upon our successful completion of Project

BS. Many, many lives will be lost, and untold damages will occur if we fail to find this rocket. Our country would incur the strongest blow in its history, and it could well be one from which she might not recover. That's about as serious as it gets. We really hate to lay this responsibility on you, but we don't see another solution. Sheriff Sterling has assured me that you will keep this project strictly confidential, not telling even your spouses and family. We have to keep everything under wraps. I know we can count on you."

Agent Short then looked to Agent King. Sammy King then said, "Thanks Cody, and thanks Sheriff Sterling. I think you have the information now that you need to get underway. The sheriff, Cody and I will be going to Cumberland as soon as we wrap up this meeting to repeat the meeting here to the five deputies there. Do you have questions?"

Deputy Kyle Potter said, "Could you describe in as much detail as possible the rocket we're looking for."

"Thank you, Deputy Potter," said Agent Short. "The Aerobee 170A is described on the sheet with the photograph that was handed out to you. It's about 40 feet long, 2 feet wide, and weighs approximately 3000 pounds. But I think I know what you're asking for, Deputy Potter. I think you would like more information about how you should go about looking for it in your surveys."

"That's correct, Agent Short," replied Kyle Potter.

"Here's what I can tell you," said Cody Short, "It could be found standing, all 40 feet of it, or it could be stored horizontally. It could even be taken apart, and only some of it standing or lying. The important thing is that it is about 2 feet in diameter, and all together weights 3000 pounds. Something of that size is really difficult to hide, but we have to assume that the bad guys have thought about this and could have come up with some clever ways to disguise it. For example, it could possibly be split in two or more lengths and those placed along the walls of a building with wooden panels constructed over them to disguise them as seats. Or they possibly could be buried in the ground, with floor coverings over them. Or they could possibly be buried outside. What I don't think you'll find is a 3000 pound, 40 feet high rocket sitting in the upright position. That would just be too easy to spot. I suggest you use your metal detectors to check out any suspicious ground disturbances you come across, or along any interior construction that could hide sections of the rocket. Other than that, I think just your intuition and training will have to suffice. One thing for certain, it's not easy to hide a rocket of this size."

"Thanks," replied Deputy Potter. "That helps."

Fred Knapp held his hand up, and was recognized by

the sheriff. Fred said, "If I could just add one comment. I know that each of you understand now the importance of this project. I just wanted to add that in addition to saving tremendous numbers of lives and preventing great damage, if you're successful this story will have a super positive impact on our county. Our country, and indeed the entire world, will understand what you accomplished, and the spotlight will be on you and Harlan County. Let me thank you in advance for all your efforts in the coming weeks."

"Thanks Fred," the sheriff said, "and thanks to each of you for being here and for your upcoming assistance. We'll have weekly progress reports at this same time, and hopefully the bad guys will be found very soon and we'll have Project BS put to bed. Thanks again."

Everyone stood and did the chit-chat for a few minutes and then left. The mayor and each deputy reached up and gave Preacher Puss a nice pet as they walked out the front door.

Bert and the two agents gathered their materials for the Cumberland meeting and departed. Bert gave the cat a gentle stroke as he walked out. The two agents saluted her.

Chapter 6

7 Months Earlier
Chincoteague, Virginia

It had been almost a month since Lee Kon had met with Geek Keelen. His superiors in North Korea were getting very worried, and were about to abort Bee Sting when they finally got word from Kon that Keelen had contacted him and requested a meeting.

Lee Kon had driven on a Saturday to the Keelen farm. Geek Keelen answered the door and invited Lee in. After exchanging a few pleasantries the two sat in the living room. Geek had gotten each a beer.

Lee Kon said, "My friend, I was about to give up on you. My contacts in North Korea were as well. I hope your asking for this meeting means that you have decided to accept the 5 million dollars!" A smile formed on Lee's face.

Geek replied, "I'm sorry it took so long, but I really had to do a lot of thinking about this. But I did, and have decided to accept your generous offer, but only under certain conditions."

"Okay," Lee said. "Let's hear 'em."

"Well, first of all, I want to do everything I possibly can to keep my identity secret. I will resign my position at Wallops saying that I have decided to move West because of a health problem. Before I do that I want your help in designing an exact duplicate of the Aerobee. It must look identical, but will not have all the electronics, etc. And it will have sand inserted for the solid fuel. Also, a control console must be developed that looks identical to the real one. I can take photographs of the rocket and the control console and give them to you along with all the physical specs. You will need to get these to North Korea and have them produce the dummy rocket and then ship it to me. They can design it such that it's in 4 lengths of 10 feet each, and that each length fits together snugly such that the mating could not be detected. Each piece could be shipped to me about a week apart....that shouldn't arouse any suspicion. So far, is that okay?"

"You have been giving this a lot of thought," Lee said. "So far, so good. What else?"

Geek continued, "I want a complete facial make over before going to Kentucky. I want a professional to change my facial appearance as much as possible, but nothing that is permanent. After this is over I want to assume my usual appearance and move West and purchase a ranch. I'll need false identity while in Kentucky. You'll have to come up with false drivers license, credit cards, and passport, just in case."

"We can do that," Lee said. "Anything else?"

"Well, there's the matter of the 5 million dollars," Geek said. "I want 1 million up front, and it will be wire transferred to an account that I'll give to you. I expect you to pay all my costs for moving to Kentucky and all expenses while there. One day before the launch of the rocket I want 3 million more dollars wire transferred to my account. And then after the launch I want the remaining 1 million transferred. Is that acceptable."

"I think so," said Lee. "I'll have to run all this by my contacts for their approval, but it all sounds okay to me. I suggest you give me a week or so to get all the approvals and then we'll get back together to talk more particulars. That okay?"

"Sure," Geek replied. "Sure is!"

• • •

2 Days Later
Pyongyang, North Korea

Kim Jong-un had just finished his noon meal. Since his boyhood schooling in Switzerland he had become extremely partial to McDonald's foods. While in Switzerland he enjoyed McDonald meals at every opportunity, and after he returned to North Korea and assumed leadership upon his father's death he ordered a crew of his chefs to go to Switzerland and learn how to duplicate the McDonald menu. They did so, taking about one month, and each gaining an average of 12 pounds. When they returned they were ordered to be on stand-by to produce anything on the McDonald menu for Chairman Kim anytime he desired it. Kim's lunch today consisted of two big Macs, 2 large orders of fries, and a large chocolate milk shake.

The door to Kim's office opened and General Ri Kwang-choi entered. He marched to Kim's desk and saluted. Kim burped and said, "Sit." General Ri took a seat on the sofa beside Kim's desk.

Kim looked at Ri and said, "General, you don't know how close you came to becoming executed. You told me that we had the rocket and this Mr. Geek Keelen all set to serve us. But it is now over a month since you told me that and you have been unable to confirm that things were in order. I understand that has changed, and you received word that Mr. Keelen has agreed to work for us and has a plan for getting the Aerobee rocket moved to Kentucky. If that is correct, then your execution will not take place. So, tell me what has happened."

A very pale General Ri spoke, "I apologize for the delay, Supreme Leader. I was led to believe that everything had been agreed to, but Mr. Geek Keelen insisted on taking some time to think through his position. Our mole, Mr. Kon, contacted me yesterday that he had again met with Mr. Keelen and that everything was back on track." Ri then went over the terms proposed by Geek Keelen and said that he felt they could put together the dummy rocket without a problem, but asked Kim for approval for the terms of paying the 5 million dollars as well as making the dummy rocket and for the cosmetic work on Geek Keelen.

The Chairman replied, "All of that is approved. What I'm interested in is getting everything moving so we can make the Thanksgiving deadline. Much has to be done to accomplish our mission in the time left. As you well know, we're now down to only about 9 months. Can it be done?"

"It will be done, Supreme Leader," General Ri replied. "We will begin immediately with getting the rocket and Mr. Keelen moved to Kentucky. In so far as moving the bomb, I have another request. I realize that Mr. Keelen is very familiar with the rocket, and will be able to launch it for us, but he is not familiar with the nuclear bomb payload. I think it will be necessary to have one of our people accompany the bomb to Kentucky, and this person will need to be very familiar with it in order to work with Mr. Keelen to properly mount it atop the rocket. With your approval, we have selected such a person. His name is Maxim Bakunin. He is called Max. He is Russian, and has been working closely with Dr. Pak Yong-ho, head of our nuclear development program. Max was sent to us by the Russians when we requested assistance with the development of our nuclear bomb program. He speaks English, although he does have an accent. Just to look at him he could easily pass as an American. We thought it necessary that all our personnel going to Kentucky be able to pass as U.S. citizens. Max's appearance can certainly do that, but he must be careful not to talk....his Russian accent would be detected. For this same reason, our mole at Wallops Island, Mr. Lee Kon will not accompany Mr. Keelen to Kentucky. Kon's appearance would not pass as native. We felt it very important that all our people involved in Project Bee Sting in Kentucky fit in as natives."

"Okay," Kim said. "I do not have a problem with this Max going to Kentucky with the bomb. How do you plan to get him and the bomb to Kentucky?"

"We have been working on that," said Ri. "We have been coordinating with Moscow to have the use of one of their advanced submarines to deliver Max and the bomb. They will rendezvous with an American fishing boat off the coast of Maine. The boat will then deliver them to a harbor where a van will be waiting. The bomb will be loaded in the van and Max will drive it to Kentucky. Of course we will supply him with false U.S. identification. His U.S. name will be Max Baker. He will meet Geek Keelen in Harlan County, Kentucky. Keelen will work out the arrangements for moving himself and the Aerobee rocket to Kentucky We should soon have all these arrangements complete."

"Very good," Kim replied. "From this point forward I expect everything to progress on schedule. You will continue to report weekly on Project Bee Sting. Of course I would expect to be told immediately of any significant development in the program. You are dismissed."

General Ri stood, saluted, and walked out of Kim's office. The chairman had a big smile on his face. He said to himself, "United States of America....soon you will be mine!"

• • •

3 Days Later
Chincoteague, Virginia

The Pony Pines restaurant was unusually quiet. It was a Thursday, and the usual crowd that gathered after work had not materialized; maybe half the normal number had drifted in for drinks and food. Earlier that day Lee Kon had contacted Geek Keelen and asked to meet after work. Lee had gotten a booth and had ordered a beer and oysters on the half shell. He was enjoying them when Geek arrived and slid into the booth.

"Did your contacts approve my requests?" Geek asked.

"If you check your bank account you'll find your balance up one million dollars," Lee said.

Geek's eyes got real big as he whispered, "I take it that means we're off and running!"

"It sure does," replied Lee. "And they want to get you to Kentucky with the rocket asap. Have you given thought to how exactly you're going to manage getting a 3000 pound, 40 foot rocket from here to Harlan County?"

Geek said, "Sure, I had a little practice when I moved it from the base to my farm. It actually breaks down into four different pieces. The booster is two pieces, each about 12 feet long, the sustainer is one 10 foot long piece, and the final piece is the payload. It's just under 6 feet long. The assembled 40 foot rocket in my barn has to lay horizontal. Lucky the barn's center aisle is almost 50 feet long! The two booster segments are the heaviest, around 900 pounds each. The sustainer weighs 600 pounds, and the payload, when loaded, another 600, but empty it's only about 100 pounds. I was able to easily manage it using a rented forklift and U-Haul truck. In addition to the rocket itself there is a control console, but it's small.....like a laptop computer. So I figure I'll rent a 15 foot U-Haul truck to load out here at the farm using a rented forklift. Do you have any idea on the timing of the dummy rocket?"

Lee said, "Yeah, they got the photographs and information you gave me and studied them carefully. They have a really good craft shop there that will be making them. Their best estimate is that it'll take about a month to make. As you suggested, they are going to make it in 4 ten foot segments, and plan to ship the first to you starting about a month from now and then one every week. So it'll likely be around 2 months until you have all four pieces."

"Good, that'll let me make plans for moving the real Aerobee. I plan to move it into the rental U-Haul and then just park it behind my house. By then everyone will know

I'm moving and a U-Haul shouldn't arouse any suspicion. Just as soon as the dummy gets here I'll set it up in the barn along with the other rockets, and then I'll move the Aerobee. Anyone coming to check on any of the museum rockets would accept the dummy as the real thing."

"That sounds fine," Lee responded. "I can tell you've been giving this a lot of thought."

"Sure have," Geek said. "So, are you going with me to Kentucky?"

Lee replied, "I wish I could. But no, I am not allowed to go. My contacts said that since I'm a native North Korean my appearance could trigger some suspicion. I must do as they say. I have a wife and two kids in North Korea and for their sake I must obey."

"I understand, but will certainly miss you. How will I be in contact with you or your North Korean contacts while in Kentucky?"

"I will be giving you a satellite phone with two quick dial numbers. The first will be to me, the second will be to one of my contacts. You will have to be very careful that the phone is not discovered. It could be traced," said Lee.

"So I think that about covers things. I've got a lot of getting ready to do," said Geek. "I'll be getting ready for the move over the next couple of months. Once the last shipment of the dummy rocket is received I should be able to travel to Kentucky within a day or so. You'll let me know the address where I will be staying in Harlan County."

"I will," Lee replied. "The location is being investigated as we speak. As soon as I know I'll let you know. In the meantime, lets have a good seafood meal here at the Pony Pines, and then we'll have lots of chances to get together to chat over the next couple of months."

Geek smiled, held up a hand and shouted, "Server!" He then looked at Lee and said, "This meal's on me!"

Chapter 7

6 Months Earlier

Pyongyang, North Korea

The meeting was about to start. Chairman Kim had gathered all those involved in Project Bee Sting to the elaborate meeting room in his Pyongyang palace.

The Chairman, sitting at the head of the long table, looked directly at General Ri Kwang-choi, sitting to his right, and said, "General Ri, it has now been about a month since Project Bee Sting was initiated. I want to know what progress has been made."

"Of course, Chairman Kim," replied General Ri as he stood to address Kim, "We appear to be exactly on schedule. Three shipments of the dummy rocket segments have been made to Mr. Keelen. The fourth and final shipment should go out this week. Upon its receipt, Mr. Keelen will move himself and the real rocket to Harlan County, Kentucky after setting up the dummy rocket in his barn, along with the others from the museum. Anyone coming to examine the rockets in his barn would certainly accept the dummy rocket as the real thing."

Kim nodded, then said, "What arrangements have been made for Mr. Keelen upon his arrival?"

General Ri then nodded to his next in command, seated across the table from him. Colonel Ju Jong-nam stood erect and said, "Mr. Chairman, General Ri, plans are in place for Mr. Keelen upon his arrival in Harlan County. Upon arriving he will stop at a grocery store located about 10 miles from Harlan. It's owner, a Mr. Green, uses the grocery store as a front for many illegal operations. Mr. Green is a friend of a Mr. Maggard, who lives in Knoxville, Tennessee. Mr. Maggard previously owned the grocery but had to sell it many years ago when he was caught in a money laundering scheme. He sold the grocery to his friend Mr. Green. We have contacts with Mr. Maggard, and have made all our arrangements through him. He has proven trustworthy in previous operations. Mr. Maggard will contact Mr. Green and employ him to carry out our needs."

Kim looked at Colonel Ju and replied, "Can we trust Mr. Green, and if so, what arrangements will be carried out by him?"

Colonel Ju continued, "Mr. Green has been checked out and seems to be acceptable. He also was highly recommended by Mr. Maggard. Mr. Green's main assistance will be two fold. First, he will assist Mr. Keelen upon his arrival, and then Mr. Max Baker when he arrives with the warhead. Secondly, he has already located and leased property in Harlan County that will be suitable for our launch site. This property is at the top of a mountain called Black Mountain. It is in the Northeastern portion of the county, and has the highest elevation in the entire state of Kentucky, some 4,145 feet."

Colonel Ju then pulled out a large map, placed it on the table facing the Chairman, and pointed out Black Mountain. The Colonel pointed to the peak and said, "As you can see, highway 160 crosses the peak of the mountain here and then goes into the state of Virginia. It is about 32 miles from the town of Harlan to the peak of Black Mountain. As the road crosses at the top there is a radar dome used for aircraft navigation off to the right, the South side of the road, on private property. Mr. Green was able to negotiate a lease with the owners of the property on the left, or North side, from the road crossing. The property is approximately 40 acres, and with a relatively flat location of about 2 acres that was suitable for construction of our building and launch site. Mr. Green signed a 99 year lease with the owner for $25,000 per year, with the first five years payable in advance. So we paid $125,000 to Mr. Green for this lease payment. Of course when the rocket is launched we will abandon the property."

Chairman Kim asked, "Under what name was the lease signed, and what was its stated purpose?"

The Colonel grinned and said, "We set up a fake corporation called Beck Signal Corporation, or BSC. The stated purpose for this lease is to erect a large antenna that will serve to send and receive signals that are government related and very confidential."

Chairman Kim nodded approvingly, then said, "I see. That sounds good. So how will the rocket launch be concealed?"

"Four very large support columns will be erected on the property. The center lines of each column will form a square 20 feet apart. Each column will be about 4 feet in diameter and 30 feet tall. The supposed purpose of these will be to form the base upon which the antenna platform will be built.. But in reality, nothing more than these four columns will be built. Three of them will be solid concrete columns. The fourth will contain a hollow center of just over 2 feet in diameter that will house the rocket."

"But the rocket is 40 feet tall," said Kim.

"Yes," replied Colonel Ju, "but there will be a hole 10 feet deep beneath the hollow column. So 10 feet of the rocket will be underground, with the remaining 30 feet above ground and enclosed in the concrete column. We thought this would be helpful in case it became known that a 40 foot rocket was missing. Anyone looking at our construction would only see four 30 feet tall columns."

Kim then asked, "But how do you explain the one hollow column to the contractors constructing it?

"We tell them the hollow core is for the cables that will connect to the antenna, and for other control cables," replied Colonel Ju

"Very good," replied Kim. "So what about office space and living quarters for our personnel?"

"Mr. Green has taken care of that for us," answered Colonel Ju. "He ordered two prefab buildings. One was for the office, the other for storage. Concrete pads were poured for the floors of both buildings. They are currently ready to be occupied. Upon his arrival, Mr. Keelen will temporarily store the four rocket components in the storage building. As soon as the hollow concrete column is ready the rocket will then be assembled and placed in the column using a large rented crane. This operation will take place at night and the road leading into the site will be blocked. Only our personnel will be present. Fortunately, Mr. Keelen knows how to operate a crane. Living quarters for Mr. Keelen and Mr. Baker have been arranged at a hotel in nearby Benham, Kentucky. The hotel is in a building that was once a school, but was converted to a nice hotel. It also serves excellent meals. We think we will need one other person to work in the office answering the phone and keeping records. Mr. Green was told that this person needed to be reliable, but not real bright. Mr. Green recommended a Mr. Bennie Sekao, who lives in Harlan. Mr. Green said Mr. Sekao is certainly not very bright, and is very reliable when he is sober. Apparently he has a little problem with alcohol, but Mr. Green said if he was being paid a good salary he would likely be okay during working hours. This was agreed to, and Mr. Sekao has been hired. He will commute daily between Harlan and the BSC site on Black Mountain. He will start as soon as Mr. Keelen has arrived."

Chairman Kim nodded in agreement and said, "Okay, so let me see if I have this right. Both buildings are now in place and ready to be occupied. The four columns are currently being erected by a construction firm. The final dummy rocket segment will be shipped this week. So within a couple of weeks Mr. Keelen should be headed for Harlan County with the rocket. Upon arrival he'll report to Mr. Green and given directions and instructions. I assume that Mr. Green will also furnish Mr. Keelen with a car, since he will be driving a rental van when he arrives."

"Correct," the Colonel replied.

The Chairman continued, "So that leaves the nuclear warhead. When will it be ready so that Mr. Max Baker can take it to Harlan County?"

General Ri looked at Dr. Pak Yong-ho, head of the North Korean nuclear development program, sitting to his right and nodded.

Dr. Pak stood and said, "Chairman Kim, Max Baker, as he will be called in the U.S., is now very much up to speed on the warhead. I have every confidence that he will be able to properly mount it on the Aerobee and set it for detonation at the rocket's apogee, or peak altitude. We have made all the arrangements with the Russian navy for transporting Mr. Baker and the warhead via submarine to the U.S. shore. They will be met by a fishing boat and the warhead and Mr. Baker taken ashore where a van will await them. After loading the warhead into the van Mr. Baker will drive it to Harlan County. He has been given directions to the BSC site. Mr. Keelen will be told in advance when to expect Mr. Baker's arrival. I think everything is all in place to get the warhead to Harlan County. Without any unforeseen problems the warhead will be ready for shipment within a month."

Kim Jong-un looked at Dr. Pak and said, "Doctor, you make sure that that bomb is ready and gets shipped on schedule."

"Yes Chairman Kim, it will be," replied Dr. Pak.

The Chairman then looked at General Ri, "I am pleased with today's report. Thus far, everything seems on schedule and without difficulties. Make sure it stays that way. You are dismissed."

General Ri, Colonel Ju, Dr. Pak, and four assistants then stood and marched out of the meeting room. Kim got a very smug look on his face and thought, Thanksgiving is going to be something very, very special for me!

Chapter 8

Present Time

October 11

Harlan, Kentucky

Sheriff Sterling and Mayor Knapp sat at a table in the front of Creech Cafe having coffee. It was early, just after 7 am. As they looked out the front window of the cafe they saw a 20 year-old, faded blue Chevy sedan passing on Central Street. Fred said, "There goes Bennie Sekao driving his mother's old car. He sure seems to be a new person now that he has a job! I just can't believe the change....from town drunk to gainfully employed citizen. What do you make of it, Bert?"

"Well, I think Bennie's a lot smarter than people give him credit for," the sheriff replied. "When he was offered a job with that new antenna company for $20 an hour he jumped on it. I know its a long commute for him, about 65 miles round trip each day, but it keeps him busy and he's making legitimate money. Probably for the first time in his life."

Mayor Knapp said, "But how did he just give up the bottle overnight? He's been the town drunk for many years. Maybe he only needed for someone to show some confidence in him. I sure wish him the best, and I hope he's able to keep staying sober and does all the work that the company assigns to him"

Bert nodded, then said, "From what he's told me all he has to do is hang around the office and answer the phone. And he said the phone seldom rings. He's also in charge of keeping records and paying bills, and he says he really enjoys that. Also, he said the other two guys there in the office frequently bring him food from the Benham Hotel. It sounds to me like he's pretty much got it made.... if he just stays off the booze."

"Well, let's keep our fingers crossed," the mayor replied. "Bennie's a good hearted soul. He deserves a break, and I hope the job continues to be real good for him. On another note, how's the survey going?"

"So far nothing," sheriff Sterling replied. "I think my guys are giving it all they have, and are doing a great job, but it's sorta like looking for a needle in a haystack. Right now we have no leads."

"The clock's ticking," the mayor said, "and I'm truly worried about what might happen if we're unable to locate that damn thing. I know we don't know exactly what kind of damage it could do, but we do know that it's important enough that the government has sent two high ranking G-men to carry out the mission. And they have told us it's vital to the national security. That scares me."

"But we've only been looking now for two days, so I think it a little premature to start thinking negatively about our chances," Bert replied. "We've still got almost 6 weeks before the Thanksgiving holiday begins. Surely we can turn up something before then."

"Hope you're right, Bert. The last thing in the world we need is for a dad-burned rocket to be fired from Harlan County soil and cause some kind of national disaster. I don't want to even think about that."

"Howdy gents, howdy, howdy," Polly squawked as she flew from her perch to the table where Bert and Fred were sitting. "Feed Polly, feed Polly." The bird walked across the table flapping her wings.

Bert reached down and got the remains of a donut and handed it to Polly. She grabbed it in her beak and swallowed in one gulp.

"Polly thanks you. Polly thanks you," the bird said, and then flew back to her perch.

Bert got a slight grin on his face and then said, "Well, Polly cheered me a bit, but one of your stories would certainly be in order, Fred."

Fred started, "You know, Bert, I did hear a real good one yesterday. A man and his wife, Ollie and Gertrude, attended the county fair every year. They were very poor, but really enjoyed checking out everything at the fair. There was a heliport there on the fairgrounds, and a pilot would take couples up in his helicopter for $50. Ollie always stopped by and talked with the pilot, but Gertrude would never agree to spend the money for a ride. She would always say, "Fifty dollars is fifty dollars." This went on for several years....Ollie would wonder over to the helicopter and start talking with the pilot. The pilot would then say, "Let me take you and the wife up for a ride. Only fifty dollars." Gertrude would always reply, "No, no. Fifty dollars is fifty dollars." Finally, one year when Ollie walked over to the helicopter the pilot said, "Hey, I'm going to make you a deal. I'll give you and the wife a free ride if you agree not to say a word during our flight. How does that sound?"

Ollie looked at the pilot and said, "You mean you'll fly us for free, and all we got to do is keep our mouths shut?"

"That's the deal," replied the pilot. "But if you say even one word you have to pay me the fifty dollars."

So Ollie and Gertrude got aboard, and off they went. The pilot figured that he'd do some loops and stunts that would scare the couple and they'd start talking. He did three full loops and then a long roll. But everything was quiet.

After landing the pilot turned and looked at Ollie and said, "You sure fooled me. I thought you'd for sure start screaming and talking when I went through those stunts."

Ollie said, "Well, when Gertrude fell out I started to say something, but then I thought, fifty dollars is fifty dollars!"

Bert started to laugh so loud that all the others in the restaurant stopped what they were doing and looked toward him. "Fred, that's the best one I've heard in a long, long time. You've certainly got me off to a good start this morning. Thank you my friend!"

As the two men stood, Fred slapped Bert on the back and said, "I'm always glad to be of help to our law enforcement."

Bert reached up and gave Polly a pet as he went out the door.

Chapter 9

5 Months Earlier
Chincoteague, Virginia

eek Keelen was sitting on the front porch of his home when he looked up and saw the FedX truck approaching down his long, unpaved driveway. The truck was followed by a large trail of dust. Geek rose from his chair and started walking to meet the truck as it approached the front of his home. The driver shouted to Geek, "Hey guy, I got another one of those long things for you."

Geek smiled, and said, "Yeah, I been looking for it. I'll give you a hand unloading it."

"Thanks," the driver replied as he jumped from his driver's seat and walked to the back of the truck. He opened the door and started pulling the 10 foot long package from the truck bed. Geek grabbed the other end and the two men walked the package to just outside the barn and laid it down.

The driver then handed Geek a pad and said, "Just sign here and I'm gone."

"Gladly," Geek replied as he signed the pad.

"You have a good day," the driver yelled as he jumped in his truck and drove off.

Geek walked back over to the barn. He had the other three dummy rocket segments in his rental van parked next to the barn. He opened the barn door, walked inside, and jumped on the rented fork lift and drove it outside. He then opened the doors on the rental van, and using the fork lift he placed the final dummy rocket segment along side the other three already in the van. He then closed and locked the van doors. His plan was to now call Lee Kon and tell him that the final piece had arrived. Lee would come over tonight, and the two of them would exchange the real Aerobee for the dummy. Geek figured the whole process should not take more than a couple of hours at most. The most time consuming part would be filling the dummy rocket with sand to make it feel as heavy as the real thing. He had already ordered a load of sand, and it was poured just outside the barn doors. The sand would have to be shoveled into the dummy rocket segments by hand. He had two large shovels stuck in the sand pile waiting. Everything was now in place. He had already packed everything he was taking with him to Kentucky into the rental van. Just as soon as they got the rockets exchanged he would lock up the place and head for Harlan County.

· · ·

Same day, after dark

Geek was again sitting in his front porch chair when he saw the lights of a car coming up his driveway. A smile formed on his face as he then recognized Lee's car. He thought, just a couple more hours and I'll be out of here with a million dollars......soon to grow to 5 million!

About a month ago Geek traveled to Norfolk for an appointment with a plastic surgeon that had been arranged by North Korea. When the doctor saw Geek, and understanding that he wished only to temporarily modify his facial appearance so that after the mission he could again assume his regular identity, he laughed. Geek had a long pony tail, a full beard, and wore thick glasses.... the typical geek look. The doctor said, "Mr. Keelen, from what I understand you wish to accomplish I really don't think you need my services. I would recommend you shave all the hair from your head, shave your beard off, and get contact lens and throw away the glasses. You will then have a completely new look. I don't think anyone would recognize you."

Geek replied, "Doctor, that just didn't occur to me. Thank you, that's just what I'll do, and after my mission I'll just let the hair grow back!" Geek had then visited an ophthalmologist and gotten contact lens. Just a couple of hours ago he shaved his head and beard and inserted the contact lens. He looked like a different person. He put his new identification cards and drivers license in his wallet. His new name during the mission was Ralph Neleek. Neleek was Keelen spelled backwards, and was chosen so that Geek could easily remember it.

Lee parked his car, jumped out, walked quickly to Geek's front porch and said, "My friend...you certainly look different! I bet you're getting ready to leave for the Bluegrass State!"

The two shook hands, and Geek said, "You got that right! All we have left to do here is move the Aerobee out of the museum, move the dummy into its place, load the Aerobee into my rental van, and then fill the dummy rocket with sand. I know we can do all that in a couple of hours, and then I leave for Kentucky. I plan to drive all night. It should take me about 14 hours. The most direct route would be to head South and go through the Chesapeake Bay Tunnel-Bridge, but I'm not going that way because the truck would be inspected before entering the tunnel. Instead I'll head North and go over the bridge to Annapolis, and then on to Kentucky. I shouldn't have any inspections that route. So if all goes well I should arrive at Maggard's Grocery sometime around noon tomorrow."

Lee said, "Boy....you'll be exhausted after that all night drive."

"Yeah," Geek said, "but I'm hoping that Mr. Green will allow me to sleep a few hours in his office before going on to the Black Mountain Site. I think it'll work out just fine."

Lee replied, "Well, let's get started. You better let me do most of the sand shoveling so you won't be too tired to drive. We sure wouldn't want you to doze off and have a wreck. What a nightmare that would be!"

Geek nodded agreement and said, "Let's get it done!"

• • •

The Following Day

1 pm

Harlan County, Kentucky

Maggard's Grocery Store is located about 10 miles South of Harlan on highway 119, near the village of Wallins, Kentucky. Built many years ago as a front for his illegal activity by Pretty Boy Maggard, and sold to Trigger Green when the law was about to catch up with Pretty Boy after confiscating his huge money laundering operation, the store continued as a front for illegal operations as directed by Trigger Green. Unlike Pretty Boy Maggard, Trigger was not bad to the core. He did engage in all kinds of illegal activities, from bootlegging to credit card fraud to stolen cars, etc., but he drew the line at causing great physical harm or death. And on occasions, he even cooperated with Sheriff Sterling in locating bad guys that were not his clients.

Trigger had his office in the back of the grocery store. The office was entered through a door that had a lock on it controlled by a button located under the counter at the grocery check- out. Trigger had one employee, Fatso Chapel, who operated the grocery store. Fatso generally could be found sitting behind the check-out counter either reading magazines or watching a small television. Fatso was famous for his fondness for corny jokes....particularly corny elephant jokes. Many that entered the store would try to avoid Fatso just so they wouldn't have to listen to one or more of his jokes. But he loved them!

Trigger walked up to the check-out counter and found Fatso dozing in his chair. His head had dropped and his chin rested on his chest. His eyes were closed. Trigger walked up to the counter and slammed his right fist down on it. Fatso jumped up several inches from his seat and said, "Trigger, I'd sure appreciate it if you'd stop doing that. I had a hard time going to sleep last night and I was just catching up a tad."

Trigger laughed and replied, "Sleeping on the job is not what I pay you to do. A bad guy could have walked right in and done anything without you even knowing it. You need to stay alert."

"Yes, boss," Fatso replied. "You know what has 8 legs, 2 trunks, 4 eyes, and 2 tails?

Trigger just looked at Fatso.

Fatso said, "Two elephants!"

"Bad," Trigger said. "I'm surprised that fellow Neleek hasn't gotten here. Pretty Boy told me to expect him around noon. Hope he didn't have trouble."

"No sign of him, boss," Fatso said. "He's suppose to be driving a rental van, isn't he?"

"Right," Trigger replied. "And when he gets here you tell him to park the van around behind the store, where it won't be seen. My guess is he'll want to catch some z's since he drove all night."

"I'll be watching for him," Fatso said. "Boss, what do elephants have that nothing else has?"

Trigger just looked at him.

"Baby elephants," said Fatso with a grin!

Trigger shook his head and started walking back to his office.

•   •   •

Fifteen minutes later

Just as he was dozing off again Fatso heard the doorbell jingle. He opened his eyes and saw a rental van parked in front of the store and a fellow just entering the door.

Fatso said, "Hey guy, I bet you're looking for Trigger Green!"

Ralph Neleek looked at Fatso and said, "That's correct. Are you Mr. Green?"

"My name's Fatso Chapel. I can direct you to Mr. Green. But first, you must tell me what was the elephant doing on the freeway?"

Ralph looked perplexed, and said, "I have no idea?"

"About 5 miles per hour," Fatso replied with a laugh. "Mr. Green's office is in the back of the store." Fatso pointed toward the office door. "Just go back to that door and knock. I'll unlock it from here." Fatso reached down and pushed the button unlocking the door.

Ralph knocked gently on the door.

"Enter," said the voice behind the door.

Ralph opened the door and walked in. Trigger rose from his desk, walked around it, extending his hand and said, "My name is Trigger Green. I'm going to guess that you are Ralph Neleek

As he shook hands Ralph said, "You would be correct, Mr. Green. I take it Mr. Maggard has been talking with you."

Trigger gestured for Ralph to have a seat, and said, "Please be seated, and let's talk."

The two talked for several minutes, going over the current status of the construction at the BSC site on Black Mountain. Trigger explained that the office and storage buildings were complete and ready to occupy, and that the four columns behind the office building were under construction. He also told Ralph that he had a room at the Benham Hotel, and handed him the room key along with keys to the office and storage buildings. Trigger then said,

"So, I think you will find everything in order." He then handed Ralph a business card. "My phone number is on the card, if you have questions or run into any trouble just give me a call. I am to assist you in any way I can."

"One other thing," Trigger said. "When you get to the office you will find another set of keys on the desk. They go to the car that is parked beside the storage building. The car is for your use while you're here. In its glove compartment you will find registration and insurance cards in your name."

"Sounds super, Mr. Green. But I do have a favor to ask. I've been driving all night and am really tired and sleepy. Is there anywhere here where I could nap for a while before going on?"

"Absolutely," replied Trigger. "I anticipated that, and have cleared out a space in our storage room and have a cot set up for you. Rest as long as you wish, but I'd advise you to get that van to the BSC site and then get back down to your hotel before dark."

"Also," Trigger added, "Please park your van around behind the grocery so it will be out of sight."

"Certainly," replied Ralph as he stood and started walking back toward the grocery store. "Thanks so much for all your help. You've covered all the bases."

"I'm well paid, my friend," replied Trigger.

As Ralph had almost reached the front door he heard Fatso yell, "Hey guy, you know why the elephant painted its toes red?"

Ralph slowed, and turned his head to look at Fatso.

"So it could hide in a cherry tree!" Fatso said with a chuckle.

Ralph moved his van behind the store and then came back in and retired to the cot in the storage room. He slept soundly for 4 hours.

• • •

Trigger shook Ralph awake and said, "Mr. Neleek, you've slept about 4 hours. You likely should get up and get the van up to the site and then drive your car down to the hotel before dark. You've still got a couple of hours of daylight left....it shouldn't be a problem."

"Okay....will do," replied Ralph. He stood, again shook hands with Trigger, thanked him for his assistance, and departed Maggard's Grocery.

Chapter 10

4 Months Earlier
in the Atlantic Ocean

The Eleanor G, a 100 foot long fishing boat based in Portland, Maine, sat dead in the water about 75 miles off the coast. It was 3 am, and there was no moon. The boat had a crew of eight. Six were sleeping. The captain, Tackett Jay, and first mate, Kip Vanaman, were sitting on the aft deck. The weather was clear, and very little wind. The sea was calm. The Eleanor G slowly swayed with the gentle rolling waves.

Captain Jay said, "Kip, my understanding was that contact was to be made tonight between 2 and 4 am. So far absolutely nothing. The Eleanor G is at the right coordinates I take it."

"Yes sir, Captain," the first mate replied. "We're exactly where we were told to be. But they've got another hour yet....I think they'll show."

"I guess," Captain Jay said. "But my eyes are beginning to droop. It's so peaceful out here, and the rocking of the boat is just about to put me to sleep."

Mate Vanaman replied, "I hear you. Same with me."

Each man took another sip of coffee and continued to stare at the dark sea.

And then it appeared. At first they heard a sound like water falling over a falls. And then there was an object in the water. It first looked like a large, round pipe coming up. And then other shapes appeared below it. The sail, or conning tower, of the submarine then came up out of the water, followed by the top of the body of the sub.....and it was huge! The 500 foot vessel slowly rose out of the water about 100 yards behind the Eleanor G. The fishing boat was dwarfed by the Soviet vessel, a Kilo-class diesel-electric attack sub, virtually silent in the water because of its electric motors and almost impossible to detect. The sub rose until it rested atop the water. A large hatch opened atop the sub and several sailors emerged. One carried a signal light and flashed the recognition code toward the Eleanor G. The first mate reached down and grabbed his light and returned the signal. Time to start the transfer.

The Captain ran to the bridge, grabbed the ship microphone, and said, "This is the captain. All hands on deck immediately. Repeat, all hands on deck."

First mate Vanaman grabbed the control panel to raise the ship's lifeboat and put it in the water. The winch first raised the craft up high enough to swing above the ship rails and then swung out over the water. It was then lowered into the sea beside the Eleanor G. The lifeboat was 25 feet long and could hold up to 40 persons. But tonight it only had to accommodate 3 plus a nuclear warhead. Captain Vanaman and his crew had only been told they were to pick up Max Baker and a 500 pound box. They did not know the box contained a nuclear warhead.

The first mate and another Eleanor G Sailor boarded the lifeboat and started it's motor. They then motored over beside the Soviet sub. Lines were then thrown over the side of the sub to secure the lifeboat. A rope ladder was then thrown down to the lifeboat, and Maxim Bakunin, aka Max Baker, came down the ladder into the boat. He shook hands and introduced himself to the first mate and said, "Now comes the hard part. The box is almost 500 pounds. It is fragile. We certainly need to be very careful moving it." The boxed warhead was contained in a web sling and four Soviet sailors slowly lowered it down the side of the sub and onto the lifeboat

The lifeboat then motored back over to the Eleanor G, and the three men climbed a ladder back aboard. The winch cables were then secured to the lifeboat and then it and the nuclear warhead were brought on board. A cover was then placed over the lifeboat to hide the warhead. This part of the mission was accomplished.

Captain Jay cranked up the motor on the Eleanor G and the fishing vessel started its journey back to port.

• • •

6 Hours Later
Portland, Maine

Captain Jay had been ordered to bring the Eleanor G into her slip at the Portland, Maine marina around noon. So he slowed his vessel to about 10 miles per hour for the 75 mile trip. All hands were on deck for docking, and the Captain at the helm slowly pulled his boat into her slip. As he did so he glanced toward shore and noticed approvingly that there was a black rental van parked where he was told it would be.

After the crew had all the lines secured Captain Jay ordered four of the crew to bring the dolly around to the lifeboat and carefully load the box onto it. This was done, and the Captain turned to Max Baker and said, "Mr. Baker my crew will help you move the box to the van and get it all loaded. You should be fine then for taking it where ever you're headed. I understand the keys to the van should be under the driver's floor mat. You have a safe trip...it was a pleasure doing business with you."

Max shook hands with the Captain and then accompanied the crew members moving the dolly to the parking lot. When they reached the van Max opened the driver's door and retrieved the keys from under the floor mat. He then opened the rear door on the van and the crew moved the boxed nuclear warhead into the van. Max thanked them, got in the van, and drove off.

Max had been given a map and directions for driving from Portland, Maine to the BSC site in Harlan County. The estimated driving time was about 21 hours. He figured he would have to stop several times for gas, food, and restroom.....so he thought he would likely arrive at the site on Black Mountain around noon the next day. Fortunately for him, he was able to get lots of rest and sleep on the sub, so he didn't think the 24 hour journey would be too taxing. He just hoped that his GPS would serve him correctly, and that he wouldn't be stopped by law enforcement. He would strictly obey all speed laws and drive very, very carefully!

. . .

The Next Day
Black Mountain, Ky.

"That Benham hotel sure knows how to cook," Bennie Sekao said as he stuffed another biscuit covered with butter into his mouth. "And I sure do appreciate you bringing me the food, Ralph."

Ralph Neleek replied, "No problem at all. They always serve twice as much as I can eat. I'm glad you enjoy it."

Ralph had gotten settled in at the BSC site a little over three weeks ago now. He hired Bennie a couple of weeks ago after getting the recommendation from Trigger Green. And Trigger was sure right....Bennie wasn't the brightest, but he had been very dependable and had shown no signs of a drinking problem since starting work. Ralph had set up a computer in the office and had shown Bennie the basics of using it. It was the first time Bennie had ever used a computer and was fascinated with it. Ralph showed him how to search for things, and had set up an email account for him. Bennie had a desk and a company phone. He had set up a filing system for office mail and paperwork, and although there were few phone calls he kept very busy playing with the computer and filing paperwork. Ralph had decided that Bennie was the perfect employee for them. He didn't have an idea what was really going on and accepted everything that Ralph told him. Ralph had explained how BSC would be building a huge antenna at the location for the purpose of transmitting and receiving very secret government information. He was told that the third employee, Max Baker, would be arriving today. Ralph said that Max was a native of Italy, and had an Italian accent, and that he would be arriving in a van that contained some very important equipment. He said that the equipment was extremely light sensitive, and for that reason they would not be unloading it until after dark. Bennie offered to stay and help but Ralph told him it was not necessary. He said the equipment was not heavy and would be no problem for the two of them to move.

The small office building had three desks. Bennie's was all set up with his computer and telephone, and he had even brought some pictures for his desk. Ralph's contained only a computer, and Max's was bare. Construction was continuing in back of the office building where the four giant concrete columns were being erected by a contractor. Ralph had been assured that the columns would be completed in about another month. The windowless storage building off to the side contained the four segments of the Aerobee rocket and its control console. The custom built prefab building had only an overhead door in front and no rear door. The overhead door opened by entering the code in a keypad beside the door on the outside. There were four security cameras located on the outside of each wall, and monitors from those cameras were mounted on one wall inside the office building. Bennie had been told by Ralph that very highly confidential and secret equipment was in the storage building and that he, Bennie, was not allowed inside since he didn't have the proper security clearance. Actually the only thing other than the Aerobee rocket and console inside the building was a rented fork lift. It awaited the arrival of the nuclear warhead.

Just as Bennie was finishing his food he glanced at one of the monitors and saw a black van pulling up beside the storage building. "Hey Ralph, I think Max has arrived."

Ralph looked up from his computer and saw Max getting out of the van and walking toward the office building. "You're right Bennie. I'm sure that's him."

Max walked into the office and said, "Greetings fellows, I'm Max Baker."

Bennie and Ralph walked over to Max, shook hands, and introduced themselves.

Bennie said, "You're right Ralph, Max does have a bit of an Italian accent."

Max smiled and replied, "I knew you'd notice. But my English is good"

Bennie said, "How about a cup of coffe, Max?"

"Yes, that sounds real good," he replied. "It's been a long haul for me. I think I'll drink a cup of coffee and then head to the hotel to get a little rest if that's okay with you guys."

"Super," said Ralph. "And after you've rested up and it gets dark why don't you drive back up here and we'll unload the equipment into the storage building. I told Bennie that it was extremely light sensitive and would have to be unloaded after dark. You can drive my car to the hotel, and I've got your room key right here." Ralph tossed a key to Max. "Your car should arrive tomorrow, we weren't sure when you would get here."

"Sure, that'll work fine," Max said as he sipped coffee. The three men chatted for another fifteen minutes and then Max departed for the hotel.

• • •

9 pm that night
Black Mountain, Kentucky

Ralph was sitting in the office with his feet propped up on his desk. He had fallen asleep. Max walked into the office and said, "Wake up Ralph....time to go to work!"

Ralph jumped up from his chair with a sheepish look on his face. He said, "Just dozing a little. It's so quiet up here after the construction crew calls it a day. Yeah, I think we need to get that bomb unloaded. I think it's dark enough that no one would notice. Let's do it."

The two men walked from the office to the storage building. Max had left Ralph's car parked in the driveway coming into the site so that no other vehicle could enter. Trees lined the road on both sides.

"I think we're good to go," Ralph said. "My car's blocking anyone from driving in, and we would see lights if they attempted to walk in."

"And it should only take us maybe 15 minutes to get it unloaded," Max said.

Ralph entered the code into the key pad for the overhead door and it rolled open. Max turned the van around and backed it up to the storage building door. Ralph cranked up the fork lift and drove it to the back of the van and then raised the forks until they were in position to go into the pallet the boxed warhead was resting on. Ralph then lifted the pallet and box, backed up, and lowered it to just about a foot off the ground. He then turned the forklift around and drove into the storage building placing the pallet in a far corner from the entrance door.

"Well, that's that," Ralph said as he jumped off the fork lift. "Everything we need is now in this storage building. Just as soon as we get those columns completed we'll be ready to assemble the thing and move it into position."

"How exactly are you planning on moving a 40 foot, 3000 pound rocket into one of those columns?" asked Max.

"No problem," Ralph replied. "We have rented an Elliott Boom Truck that has a boom with a 105 foot length. It's scheduled to be delivered to us in a couple of weeks. It should raise no suspicion since we're supposedly in the process of building this antenna platform. Once the Aerobee is assembled in the horizontal position we'll use a harness attached to the upper part of the rocket to raise her with the crane and then slowly, slowly drop her into the column. Should work like a charm. But of course we'll have to do all that one very dark night!"

Max nodded in agreement. The two men lowered the storage building door, locked up the office, got in Ralph's car and headed for the Benham Hotel. It had been a full day!

Chapter 11

3 Months Earlier
Black Mountain, Kntucky

    Bennie, Ralph, and Max each sat at their desk in the BSC office building. It was mid morning. Bennie was playing with his computer, Max was studying a report, and Ralph was daydreaming about how he was going to live after this mission was over and he had 5 million dollars in his bank account. The construction of the columns out back was still fully underway, and now the contractors had said that because of some problems they had encountered it would likely be about another month before finishing.

    Max glanced at the monitors on the wall and suddenly jumped up from his seat with an excited look on his face.

He said, "Hey guys, it looks like we've got law enforcement visitors."

Bennie and Ralph both looked at the monitor. Ralph turned pale, but said nothing. Bennie said, "Oh, that's nothing to worry about. That's my friend Sheriff Sterling. He said he was going to stop by one day to see what we were up to!"

Max turned pale, and Ralph turned even paler.

Bennie said, "Hey guys....something wrong? You two don't look so good!"

Ralph said, "We're fine, we just were startled to see the police car. You say he's your friend?"

"Well, let's just say we know each other pretty well. In my former life we frequently encountered each other. He's a nice guy. You've got nothing to worry about. He's just stopping by to be friendly."

There was a knock on the door. Bennie ran to open it.

"Hi Bennie, good to see you again. I just thought I'd drop in to see you and to meet the others up here. Just a social visit....nothing official!"

"Hey Bert," Bennie replied. "It's really good to see you. You told me a few weeks back that you would visit us. I appreciate your driving all the way up here. Let me introduce my bosses.....Ralph NeleeK and Max Baker."

The sheriff shook hands with Ralph and Max. Ralph said, "Sheriff, it's a pleasure to meet you. Bennie has told us what a great guy you are. Bennie here has proven to be a super employee for us. We appreciate him a lot." Max nodded agreement.

Bennie pulled up another chair for the sheriff and said, "Have a seat Bert.....can I get you a cup of coffee?"

"I never turn down a cup of mud," Bert replied. "Just black will be fine, thanks."

Bennie gave Bert his coffee and the sheriff said, "You guys are sure well underway here with a large project. I understand it has something to do with construction of a big antenna. I saw the four huge columns going up out back. I assume they will support the antenna?"

Ralph replied, "That's correct sheriff. A platform with be built on top of the columns that will be the support for the antenna."

"I see," Bert replied. "And what exactly is the purpose of the antenna?"

Ralph said, "I mean no disrespect sheriff, but because of security issues we can't talk about the specifics of our operation. I can tell you that we will be receiving and sending signals that are confidential, and some top secret. They come from various agencies in our government, and some from friendly foreign governments. BSC is simply the operating contractor to get the station up and going."

"And when do you anticipate that will be?" Bert asked.

"Good question," replied Ralph. "The contractors building our columns keep encountering delays. Right now they say that the columns should be finished within the next month. We'll then start to move into the phase to build the platform, and finally the antenna. The platform will likely take about 3 months to build, and then the antenna is pretty much prefabed. If all goes well we should be up and running by the middle of next year."

"Max, you've been very quiet," the sheriff said.

Max said, "Yes, my English is not real good. I'm originally from Italy, but have been employed with BSC for about 5 years."

"I understand," Bert said. "Well, I don't want to keep you guys from your work. I just wanted to stop by to say hello. Ole Bennie here goes back a long way with me, and I'm really pleased that you employed him and that he is working out so well for you." Bert finished his coffee and stood up.

"Sheriff, we thank you for stopping by. Our door's always open, and we hope to make a strong contribution to the economy of Harlan County," Ralph said.

The three men shook hands. Bennie slapped Bert on the back and said, "I really do appreciate you Bert. Thanks so much for thinking about me. I'll see you in town before long I'm sure. You be careful driving back down Black Mountain."

"Thanks Bennie. You guys have a good day," The sheriff said as he walked out the door to his cruiser.

Bennie then looked at the other two and said, "See, I told you he was a nice guy. Just paying us a social visit."

Max then said, "Yes, but we want you to be very careful when talking with the sheriff. Don't talk about BSC business. It's very confidential." Ralph nodded in agreement.

Bennie said, "My lips are sealed. Except when you bring me some more of that good food from the Benham Hotel!"

The three men looked at the monitor and watched as Sheriff Sterling turned his cruiser around and left the site. Ralph and Max looked at each other and got slight grins on their faces as the color returned to them.

• • •

That Afternoon
Harlan, Kentucky

"So ole Bennie seems to be doing fine?" Fred Knapp asked Sheriff Sterling as the two sipped iced tea in Creech Cafe.

Bert replied, "So it would seem. He's got a desk, and even a computer! He's stone sober, and the guys he works for seem to like him a lot. Bennie's got a lot to be thankful for."

"What was your take on the big antenna going up?" the mayor asked.

"Oh they're making good progress. Four huge concrete columns 25 or 30 feet high are about to be completed, and then they'll proceed to build a platform on the columns for the antenna. They said it should be completed sometime around the middle of next year. But you know how construction projects go."

The mayor then said, "Did you find out what the purpose of the antenna was?"

Bert said, "Only that it involved sending and receiving information for government agencies. They said it was very confidential, and couldn't talk much about it. BSC is simply the operating contractor."

"Sounds like they're spending a lot of our tax payer money, if you ask me," Fred replied with a chuckle.

"Well, at least it's being spent in Harlan County," Bert replied, "and Lord knows our economy needs it!"

Fred said, "You sure got that right!"

Bert looked over at the wall to his right and said, "Fred, that looks like a new posting on your wall. What's the story behind it? It looks like a photo of a guy crying beside a grave stone."

Fred laughed and said, "Yeah, I just put that one up a couple of days ago. It was published in the Harlan Daily Enterprise. What happened was this man went to the cemetery to visit his family plot. As he was walking to it he passed a grave stone that had a fellow on his knees holding to the stone and saying, 'Why did you have to die? Why did you have to die?'. The man stopped and said to the fellow, 'This must have been someone you loved very much.' The fellow looked up and said, 'No, I never met him....he was my wife's first husband!'"

Bert roared with laughter, stood up and said to Fred, "That's a jewel. Thanks for sharing it." The sheriff walked out the door headed across the street to his office.

• • •

The Next Morning
Benham Hotel
Benham, Kentucky

It was 6:30 am. Ralph and Max were having breakfast at their hotel in Benham. The two sat at a table isolated from others in the dining room. Ralph said, "Max, when I saw that police cruiser yesterday I thought I was going to faint. I can't remember when I felt so scared."

"I felt the same way," Max said. "I just figured that they had somehow gotten onto us and we were getting ready to be arrested."

Ralph replied, "Yeah, I know. I just hope that our feelings didn't show when the sheriff met us. When Bennie explained that he had actually invited him for a visit I began to feel a little better, but I'm sure I likely still looked a little pale."

"Well, the good news is that either the sheriff is an extremely good actor, or else he didn't detect our feelings," Max said. "I think we passed the test. And I think he bought our story about BSC."

"I think so," said Ralph. "Hopefully since he made the visit we won't be bothered again by him or any of his deputies."

The two finished their breakfast and left for Black Mountain.

Chapter 12

Present Time

October 19

Oval Office, Washington, D.C.

Six were assembled for the meeting in the White House. In addition to President DeVore, CIA Director Rudy Lester, Secretary of Defense Sam Back, and Secretary of Homeland Security Josh Dillon, FBI Special Agent Sammy King and CIA agent Cody Short were present.

President DeVore said, "Gentlemen, I thank you for adjusting your schedules to meet with me today. It has now been two weeks since we began what has now been labeled project BS. I know that each of you realize the extreme importance of locating the rocket and eliminating the threat to our country. I asked Agents King and Short to meet with us since they have firsthand knowledge of our activity in Harlan County." The President then nodded at the agents.

Agent Short began, "Thank you Mr. President. Sammy and I are pleased to share with you all we know up to this point. As you stated Mr. President, it has only been two weeks since we got Project BS underway." He went on to relate to the group all the activities that had taken place, leaving out the encounter with Preacher Puss."

"So the Sheriff's Department is currently conducting this county wide search, but there has been nothing suspicious detected so far?" President DeVore asked.

Agent King replied, "That's right, Mr. President. Cody and I have great confidence in Sheriff Sterling and his men, and we think they are working very hard to locate the rocket."

Josh Dillon said, "We understand that, but we also understand that as of today we only have a little over 5 weeks before the Thanksgiving holidays. Do either of you have any recommendations for additional assistance to help locate the rocket?"

"We've thought about that a lot," replied Cody Short. "And we've not been able to think of anything additional that could be done at present without revealing the nature of the mission and scaring everyone in Harlan County. If we come up with something we'll certainly make the request."

The President and his team all nodded in agreement.

President DeVore then said, "Very well....we continue on. But before we adjourn I'd like you two agents to hear a brief report about our activity here for the past couple of weeks." The president looked at Rudy Lester and nodded.

The CIA Director said, "We have been busy trying to identify any activity that could be associated with Project BS. First, we have been making a thorough search of all U.S. facilities that stock any kind of rocket that could be used to deliver the payload. There are lots of such locations. So far we have been able to account for all our inventory, but we're still looking. Of course it could well be that the rocket they're going to use is not one of ours, but if that's the case we have no way of knowing. The second thing I wanted to report to you is that we've been very actively investigating all border activity over the past year that could reveal where the bomb and/or rocket might have been imported. As I know you realize, this is certainly like looking for the ole needle in the haystack.... but we've got to try. We're hoping that we'll just get lucky and someone will have noticed something suspicious that will help us. We'll continue these two efforts vigorously."

"Thanks Rudy," President DeVore said. "So I guess that's about it for present. Again, I appreciate so much the efforts from each of you. Keep at it. You know how important this thing is, and how much our country is counting on you. We'll stand adjourned until something develops that justifies another meeting. Thanks guys!"

And in unison the other five said, "Thank you Mr. President."

• • •

Same Time
BSC office
Black Mountain, Kentucky

Max and Ralph sat at their desks. Bennie had been sent on an errand into Harlan. No one else was in the office.

Ralph said, "I'm sure happy I'm not really in the construction business. Those jerks building our columns have now managed to fall behind schedule by yet another month. Fortunately for us, we started their construction early enough that we're still okay. I could not imagine any reason why they wouldn't be finished up within the next week or so. We've still got 39 days before Wednesday,

November 27th. At least the delay with the columns gives us an excuse for not getting underway with the platform construction. So I guess we're okay."

Max replied, "It should work. I'm going to need some time integrating the payload onto the rocket, but that shouldn't take more than a couple of days. When time gets close to lifting the rocket into position I'll start mating the payload with the sustainer stage. I can do that in the storage building. Yeah, I think everything is proceeding okay. I'm mostly worried about some kind of inspection from the police."

"Bennie said he's not been talking to anyone about our operation," Ralph replied. "And I do think we can trust him. But like you, I have a feeling that officials are aware of something going on, and I bet they're trying to locate us. I'm just glad we've not been discovered so far. I guess our cover is working. But I sure will be happy to see Thanksgiving this year!"

Max nodded, and each man returned to their computer.

• • •

Same Time

Harlan, Kentucky

Fred Knapp was standing at the cash register at Creech Cafe. Polly was sitting on her perch beside Fred. Fred was gently stroking the bird. Fred looked out the front window and saw Bennie Sekao walking down Central Street approaching Creech Cafe. Fred ran to the door, opened it, and shouted, "Hey Bennie....come in here."

Bennie waved to Fred and said, "Sure thing Mr. Mayor". He walked to Fred and slapped him on his back. The two entered the store, found a table, and sat.

Fred said, "What are you doing in Harlan. At this time of the day I'd have thought you'd be on top of Black Mountain hard at work."

Bennie grinned and said, "Mayor, I was sent to Harlan to pick up some supplies. I guess my job description includes being a 'gofer', but I don't mind at all. It gives me a chance to get out of the office and enjoy some of this delightful weather."

"Well you're certainly looking great, Bennie. I just can't get over the change in you since you got that job. I'm really, really proud of you."

"You know Mr. Mayor," Bennie said, "I really do feel good about myself now. When I was the town drunk

I only felt good when I was drinking, which was a good part of the time. But when I wasn't drinking I felt really terrible. Now that I've been sober, I feel good 100% of the time."

"Like I say, Bennie, I'm proud of you. Keep it up. So how's everything going up on Black Mountain?"

Bennie said, "Well, to tell the truth, it's been a bit slow. Those doggone contractors building those big concrete columns are really behind schedule.....and that's slowed things down considerably."

The mayor thought a minute, and said, "Bennie, how tall are those columns?"

"Thirty feet, exactly," he replied.

The mayor stroked his chin, and said, "Just 30 feet?"

"Yep.....exactly 30 feet," Bennie replied.

"Mr. Mayor, I gotta run. I wanted to stop by and say hi to the sheriff, and then I got a few more things I have to pick up at Wal-Mart."

"Sure, Bennie, I understand. Let me tell you one I heard on the radio this morning."

Bennie got a smile on his face.

Fred said, "This preacher came to a small town in Kentucky to hold a revival. He had something he wanted to mail, and as he was walking down the street he stopped a small boy and asked him how to find the post office.

The boy gave him directions, and the preacher said, 'Son, come to the Baptist church tonight and you'll hear me tell everyone how to get to heaven'. The boy said, 'Preacher, I don't think I'll be there. You didn't even know how to get to the post office!'"

Bennie and Fred laughed aloud, and Bennie said, "Another jewel, Mr. Mayor. Thanks. See you later." And Bennie started across the street toward the Sheriff's Department.

• • •

As Bennie walked in the door he looked up at Preacher Puss and got a frown on his face. Then he heard Rosie say, "Well, well, if it isn't Mr. Bennie Sekao. And I must say, you're looking the best I've ever seen. That new job is certainly agreeing well with you."

"Hi Rosie," Bennie said. "Still got that damn cat, I see."

"Oh Bennie, Preacher Puss is a darling. You've just had some bad luck with her in the past. As long as you don't draw any guns around her you'll be fine. Isn't that right Preacher Puss?"

The cat stood, swished her tail, and purred loudly.

Rosie said, "See, she wants to make up with you!"

"Never mind that, Rosie. Could I please say hi to Bert?"

"Certainly," Rosie replied, and the two of them walked to the door to the sheriff's office.
Rosie knocked, cracked the door and said, "Bert, you got a visitor."

The sheriff stood and walked around to the door, saw Bennie, and said, "Bennie, my friend, please do come in. Have a seat."

Bennie said, "No Bert, I just wanted to say hi. I'm in town on some errands for BSC. I just chatted a moment with the mayor, and wanted to say hi to you. Hope everything is going well."

"Fine, thanks, Bennie," the sheriff replied. "You guys got those columns all finished yet?"

"Ha Ha," Bennie said. "The contractor says they're about there, but they still are not completed. I think maybe another week."

Bert said, "Bennie, when I was up there I saw the columns and it looked then like they were about 25 feet tall. Was I close?"

"Off by about 5 feet, Bert. They are each exactly 30 feet tall"

Bert thought for a moment, then said, "Well, thanks for stopping by. The whole town is really proud of you Bennie. You keep up the good work, and I'll see you soon again."

The two shook hands and Bennie walked back into the front office. He said to Rosie, "Thanks, Rosie, I enjoyed chatting with you, but that cat and me are still not friends!"

Rosie laughed. As Bennie went out the door he stuck out his tongue at Preacher Puss. The cat hissed and meowed at him.

• • •

3 Hours Later
BSC office
Black Mountain, Kentucky

Max and Ralph were sitting at their desks. Ralph looked up at the monitors and said, "Well, it looks like Bennie's back."

Max replied, "Yep. Hope he got all our supplies."

Bennie walked in the door with large grocery bags in each arm. "Hi guys. I think I was able to get everything. Even had a chance to say hi to the mayor and the sheriff." He placed the bags down on a table.

Max and Bert looked at each other. Ralph said, "Oh, you talked with the mayor and sheriff? What did they have to say?"

"Nothing much," Bennie replied. "We just did the chit-chat for a bit." Bennie then got a puzzled look on his face, and added, "But come to think of it, both of them asked about the column construction and each seemed real interested to know exactly how high the columns were."

Max said, "Wonder why they wanted to know that?"

Bennie replied, "Couldn't tell you. But all I told them was that they were 30 feet tall."

Ralph looked again at Max and said, "Max, I need to show you something. Would you mind stepping outside?"

The two men walked outside the office building. Ralph pointed toward the storage building and said, "We've got to do something to hide those rocket parts. I get the feeling that the mayor and sheriff asked how high the columns were for a very good reason. Maybe they know how long the rocket is?"

Max said, "Well, if they do they know it's 40 feet and those columns are just 30. So we should be safe."

"I don't think so," Ralph said. "They know the rocket could be stored in sections. And they know we have this storage building. My guess would be that they are going to be coming to inspect inside the storage building in the near future. We've got to figure a way to hide everything in there other than the fork lift."

"You could be right," Max said. "Why don't we think about it and then hang around after Bennie has left work today and talk about what we might be able to do?"

Ralph said, "Good idea."

• • •

The two looked at the monitors and saw Bennie's car drive away from the site.

Max said, "Well, let's talk. You got any ideas how we might hide it?"

Ralph replied, "I do. I think we need to build a false wall inside the storage building and store all the rocket segments, the control panel, and the warhead behind the wall. It would only have to be about 2 feet wide to accommodate everything. All the rocket segments and the warhead are 2 feet in diameter, so if we make the false wall only about 25 inches wide everything will fit in. We can mount shelve brackets onto the inside wall so that we can stack the rocket parts. The bracket rows would only have to be about 30 inches apart. The first rocket segment could lay on the floor and then the others on the brackets one above the other. We will only need four rows of brackets.

And I would suggest we put the false wall on the very back of the building. The building is 25 feet square. So if we put up the false wall on the very back it would only reduce that dimension by 25 inches plus the thickness of the wall material. So only about 26 inches. I don't think anyone would notice it. What's your thought?"

Max said, "Boy, you did do a lot of thinking about it. I think it's a super idea. Fortunately the inside walls are already finished out in plywood, so we just use plywood for the false wall and it'll look identical. When do we start?"

"I think we need to make a list of materials and send Bennie to the lumber yard tomorrow morning first thing. We'll tell Bennie we're working on some of the equipment in the storage building. He'll buy that....it won't arouse any suspicion," said Ralph

"Good idea," replied Max. "The lumber yard should be able to deliver the materials before noon, and we can get underway. Hopefully be able to finish it tomorrow....might have to work a little overtime!"

Ralph nodded and said, "Let's get that list made."

Chapter 13

Present Time

October 21

Harlan County, Kentucky

Trigger Green walked up to the check-out counter and said to Fatso Chapel, "I've had a lot of really strange requests, but the one I just got tops them all."

Fatso looked up from his magazine and said, "Oh, and what was that Trigger?"

"Pretty Boy Maggard just called me and said he wanted four large boxes of electronic equipment and 4 pieces of 12 inch diameter steel pipe 10 feet long delivered to the BSC Black Mountain site asap."

"That is weird," Fatso replied. "What kind of electronic stuff?"

"That's the really weird part. He said it didn't matter. It could even be used junk, but it needed to be electronic and it needed to look impressive. He said if we couldn't round up enough suitable junk quickly to go ahead and buy new stuff. He just said he needed it quickly."

"Okay. I guess we could come up with it. What do you suggest?" Fatso asked.

"How about if you go to the junk yard and look around. Take some boxes with you and gather up anything that looks electronic. I'll call and order the pipe. When you get back we'll look at what you've got and go from there."

Fatso said, "Okay, but you'll have to mind the store." Then he added, "You know what you call an elephant with an extra long nose?"

"I think it's called a trunk," replied Trigger. "But, no, I do not know!"

"A smellephant," replied Fatso.

"Get out of here, Fatso. I'll mind the store. And get back here as quickly as you can...Pretty Boy sure sounded like it was urgent, and he said not to worry about the cost. And he's paying us handsomely for our trouble."

"I'm outta here boss"

. . .

3 Hours Later

Trigger Green was dozing at the check-out counter when he heard the doorbell jingle. He looked up to see Fatso walking toward him with a big grin on his face.

"What's that grin all about?" Trigger asked.

Fatso replied, "Got lucky. I went to Sam's Junk Yard. Ole Sam does a pretty good job of sorting things out. When I told him I was looking for electronic stuff he directed me to a building where he had a massive pile of all kinds of electronic gadgets. I got my boxes and started picking through it. Everything that looked real good and impressive I got. I searched through that junk for almost two hours. My car has four boxes full of it. Sam just charged me by the pound. It amounted to 220 pounds for all four boxes, and I paid him $330....it was $1.50 per pound. I hope that was okay."

Trigger said, "Man, that's better than okay." Trigger reached in his pocket for a wad of money and peeled out $500 and handed it to Fatso.

"Thanks boss....you're a generous soul."

"Now what I want you to do is drive around back and take a stack of small boxes from our supply room. Put those electronic gizmos in boxes and tape them shut. Then put all the small boxes back into the big boxes and tape them up. So we'll wind up with four large boxes all taped up, and inside each will be a whole bunch of smaller boxes taped up with electronic gadgets in each one. Got it?"

"Yeah, I got it. But first you gotta tell me what's big and grey with horns?"

Trigger stared at Fatso.

Fatso chuckled and said, "An elephant marching band!"

"Get going before I take that $500 back," shouted Trigger.

Trigger pulled out his cell phone and called Pretty Boy Maggard. "Hey Pretty Boy, we got the electronic junk. Fatso's packing it up now. Four big boxes, each with many small boxes inside. Each one has electronic gear in it and is taped shut. I've called and ordered the pipe. I'll borrow a truck first thing in the morning and load the boxes and pick up the pipe and have Fatso deliver them to BSC. How's that for asap?"

Pretty Boy replied, "Good, good. I knew I could count on you. I'll deposit $10,000 for your trouble. It should show up on your bank account later this evening. That good?"

"Perfect," Trigger said.

. . .

Next Day, October 22
BSC office
Black Mountain, Kentucky

It was 11 am. Ralph and Max had worked the previous two evenings from about 6 till midnight building the false wall in the back of the storage building. They were both very tired, but had finished the wall last night. They slept a little later this morning, not getting to work until around 10 am. Bennie had given them a hard time about keeping bankers hours.

Bennie looked to the monitors and saw a truck approaching. "Hey guys, looks like we got some kind of delivery. Are the construction guys expecting anything?"

"No," replied Ralph. "That's ours. Trigger Green helped us get some parts and equipment we needed. That's likely Fatso driving the truck."

Bennie got a worried look on his face, and said, "I know Trigger Green. He's really a pretty good guy, but I know he runs a very illegal operation. Why would BSC be doing business with him?"

Ralph said, "Because he has lots of contacts and can get things really quickly. We had some parts and equipment we need really fast. Normal delivery was going to take forever. He was recommended to us. We called him and he was able to get everything we needed and deliver it within 24 hours. And there was nothing illegal about it."

"Oh....okay, I understand. Now I feel better. I really like ole Fatso. It'll be good to see him, but I do dread having to listen to one of his corny jokes," Bennie said with a chuckle. All three men walked outside to meet Fatso.

Fatso parked the truck, jumped out, and said, "Hey Bennie, good to see you. I've got some stuff to deliver."

Bennie said, "Hey Fatso. Good to see you. I want you to meet my bosses here. Ralph Neleek and Max Baker."

Ralph winked at Fatso, having met him previously on his way in, shook his hand, and said, "Nice to meet you Fatso."

Max shook hands with Fatso and said, "Real good to meet you."

Ralph then said, "Fatso, if you would be so kind as to back the truck up to the storage building door. Max and I will unload the stuff into the storage building. You can stay here and talk with Bennie....because of security reasons we can't let anyone in the storage building, I hope you understand."

"No problem at all, Ralph," Fatso replied. "I sure don't mind not unloading that stuff, and I'll enjoy talking with ole Bennie....we go a long way back!"

Fatso parked the back of the truck next to the storage building door, then jumped out and walked back down to the office building. He and Bennie then went inside to sit and chat. Max and Ralph walked to the storage building, opened the overhead door, and started unloading the boxes and pipe.

After about 15 minutes Ralph and Max walked back into the office building.

Bennie said, "That didn't take long. Fatso and I have been enjoying getting caught up."

Fatso said, "Yeah, we sure have." Fatso then handed Bennie a clipboard for his signature, receiving the shipment, and then an invoice. "Been a pleasure meeting you two, and really good to have a chance to chat with ole Bennie. But before I go, you gotta tell me what you get when an elephant skydives?

Bennie chuckled. Ralph and Max looked perplexed.

Fatso said, "You get a big hole!"

Ralph and Max shrugged their shoulders. Bennie slapped Fatso on the back and said, "Fatso, you need to write a book of those corny jokes."

Fatso grinned, nodded, turned, and walked out the door.

• • •

Later that day

Bennie looked at the clock on the wall and said, "Hey guys, it's quitting time. I'm off this mountain. See you boys tomorrow."

The two looked at Bennie. Ralph said, "See you Bennie. Max and I will stay for a while.....we got in a little late this morning."

"Don't work too hard," Bennie said as he walked out the door. Max and Ralph watched on the monitors as he got in his car and left.

Ralph then said, "Max, that was a brilliant idea you had. After we got that false back wall all finished and all the rocket stuff stowed in it, that just left the fork lift in view in the storage building. If the law had come looking they certainly would have thought it strange that we had such a secure building just for a fork lift. Now if they come, they'll find the pipe and the boxes, and if they open the boxes they'll just find electronic equipment. We'll just say it is highly confidential, but has to do with being installed onto the antenna. That should stump em. I feel like we really got our bases covered now."

Max said, "Yes indeed. I feel the same way. We'll sleep well tonight!!"

Chapter 14

Present Time

October 27

Pyongyang, North Korea

General Ri looked tense as he stood before Chairman Kim's desk. Kim said, "General, today marks exactly one month before our Bee Sting strike. I wanted to check with you to make sure that everything was on track."

"Indeed, Mr. Chairman," the general replied. "As you know, the primary feedback we get from Kentucky is through Max Baker. We know we can trust him, and we're less certain about Geek Keelen, aka Ralph Neleek. Baker reports to us regularly using his satellite cell phone, usually at night in Kentucky and from his hotel room. Everything he tells us seems to confirm that all is going well. The concrete columns will be completed in the next couple of days, and the rocket has been hidden in a storage building by stacking it's sections one above the other behind a false wall only a little over 2 feet thick. Just in case the police decide to search the storage building we have moved 4 boxes of electronic gear and 4 long pieces of pipe into it. That should provide cover. When we're ready to move the rocket into the hollow column the false wall will be removed, the rocket assembled, and then a rented boom truck will lift the rocket and place it in the column. Mr. Baker says that everything looks good at present.

He said they suspect that law enforcement is looking for the rocket, but this is just a suspicion. They don't know for sure."

Kim nodded, and said, "I understand. Do we know anything more about any search being made for the rocket?"

General Ri replied, "Nothing concrete. We learned from Mr. Maggard that Trigger Green told him the sheriff's deputies are searching the county for a large shipment of illegal drugs, but we have no reason to think that is connected to our mission Bee Sting."

"What is the plan for Baker and Neleek to escape after the rocket is fired," the Chairman asked.

The general said, "We have made arrangements with Trigger Green to deliver two old cars to the BSC site several days before the rocket launch. The cars will be old enough that they do not have electronic components, and therefore will not be effected by the electromagnetic pulse from the nuclear explosion. We have been assured by Mr. Green that two such cars will be located and that they will be in good running condition. After the launch Neleek will take one car and drive West. I think he plans on getting a ranch and then assuming his real idenity. Mr. Baker will drive the other car to Atlanta, Georgia and wait until airline operations are again up and running. When that happens he will fly home."

"Okay," Kim said, "all that sounds good. Is there anything else we should be doing now?"

General Ri replied, "Mr. Chairman, I think not. We will continue to monitor everything and I will report any needs that develop."

"Very well, you are dismissed."

General Ri turned and walked out of the office. Chairman Kim reached down and pushed the intercom button to his secretary, "I want 3 Big Mac's, two orders of large fries and a large chocolate milkshake. And I want it fast."

"Yes Chairman Kim," came the reply. Kim sat back in his chair and started daydreaming. First about the upcoming Thanksgiving eve rocket shot, and then about the delicious McDonald's meal that was on its way. A large smile formed on his face.

• • •

Present Time, Next Day
October 28
Harlan, Kentucky

It was Monday morning. Sheriff Sterling sat in his office. With him were Chief Deputy Kyle Potter and Mayor Fred Knapp.

The sheriff said, "Guys, we are now within a month of the Thanksgiving holiday. And sad to say, our search has produced zilch. I am certainly now getting concerned. I know we've still got almost a month, but I sure don't like running it down to the wire. Any ideas at all?"

Deputy Potter spoke, "Obviously we need to continue the search, and hopefully it will ultimately produce results. But I did have a couple of thoughts about additional surveillance. I know that the feds had planes and choppers looking from the air at the beginning of

Project BS, but that was a while ago. Maybe things have changed now with the rocket and possibly it could now be visible from the air. What do you think about asking for them to do another flyover of the county? The other thought I had was this. I know we don't know the nature of the bomb that the rocket will carry, but I'm betting it's a nuke. Otherwise, why would the feds be this interested in it? If that's the case, maybe we should get our hands on some Geiger counters. I know the office has one, a Radex RD1503 Dosimeter, but if you thought this a good idea we would need 11 more. They cost $167 each, so that would be $1837. Maybe the feds would foot the bill. What do you think?"

The mayor spoke, "I'll speak for myself, Kyle, and I agree completely with both ideas. I think Bert should request the repeated air search and 11 more of those counters from the feds."

Bert replied, "Kyle didn't go to Eastern Kentucky University's law enforcement school for nothing! I think those are excellent ideas. Just as soon as our meeting is over I'll call the feds and make the request. I certainly don't think they would object. They have to suspect that we suspect a nuclear warhead. What will be very important will be to make sure that all our deputies are aware that when they use the Geiger counters they not let anyone know what it is. Using a dosimeter to try and detect nuclear radiation in no way fits our cover story of looking for drugs. They could just say they were 'drug sniffers'. No one would know the difference. We can emphasize this point in our meeting when we distribute them. Thanks Kyle. Really good thinking."

Fred stood up and slapped Kyle on the back and said, "Boy, you got a good head on them shoulders!"

Kyle blushed and replied, "Glad you guys liked the ideas. I just hope we can turn up something soon!"

• • •

Same Day

CIA Headquarters, George Bush Center for Intelligence
Langley, Virginia

CIA Director Rudy Lester sat beside Technician Bobby Travis. The two were glued to a monitor that showed a very faint image that had been recorded by a U.S. satellite about 4 months ago. Travis was one of 20 technicians that had the job of viewing satellite data looking for anything unusual along the U.S. coast. His area was up to 100 miles off the coast of Maine. It was extremely tedious and slow work, and for that reason what they were now interested in was 4 months old. The satellite pass had picked up a faint image on a night when there was no moon and at around 3:15 in the morning. The image they were looking at was that shown from a night vision lens. At first pass Travis had almost missed it, but then he noticed a few pinpoints of light, indicating the presence of personnel. He had enlarged and enhanced the image, and that was when he clearly saw the outline of what looked to be a fishing boat parked beside a huge cigar-shaped vessel....undoubtedly a submarine. He then checked the location of all U.S. subs and verified that none were in that area. It was a foreign vessel. The enlarged and enhanced picture clearly showed 4 persons standing outside the sub and a smaller vessel, likely the lifeboat from the fishing vessel, secured to the side of the sub. The video clip then showed something being brought out of one of the sub's hatches and passed using a sling net down to the lifeboat. They then saw one person leave the sub and pass down to the lifeboat joining two others, along with whatever was in the sling net. Director Lester and Travis had replayed this video clip about 20 times trying to get additional information from it. But one thing was for sure, a foreign submarine and fishing vessel had met and one person along with some kind of gear was transferred from the sub to the lifeboat and then to the fishing vessel.

Rudy Lester said, "Bobby, I think we've gotten everything we can get from this clip. I think it must be something super important to involve a foreign sub. You say you have now tracked the fishing boat after the transfer and it traveled to Portland?"

"Affirmative, Mr. Lester. And by the time it reached port it was mid-day, so I could easily tell the slip it entered. I have that information written down right here. As soon as I got this I called my superior and he called you. That's where we stand right now. We can identify the slip where the fishing boat tied up, and from that I'm sure you can get an id on the fishing boat. And just as soon as they docked they took the crate from the covered lifeboat and moved it to a black van that was parked at the marina. One person got in the van and drove off. That's about all we can do for you."

"And that's plenty, Bobby. Please make me a copy of that video clip of the transfer. No need to give me the passage video as the boat makes its way back to Portland. But when it gets in the slip give me a copy of that....is that possible?"

Technician Travis replied, "No problem. Give me about an hour."

Rudy Lester then pulled out his cell phone and called his secretary. He asked her to set up a meeting with the President for later that day.

• • •

Later That Same Day
White House Situation Room
Washington, D.C.

It was 6 pm. Assembled in the John F. Kennedy Conference Room, commonly called the Situation Room, in the basement of the West Wing of the White House were Rudy Lester, Sam Back, Josh Dillon, and President Thomas DeVore.

The president said, "Gentlemen, I thank you for gathering on such short notice, but I received a call from Rudy that seemed important enough that we should meet. We're here in the Situation Room because Rudy has some video clips he wants to show. Rudy."

The CIA Director then described what his technician Bobby Travis had discovered. After showing the video clips from the satellite he said, "Obviously we can't see detail of the people or what's in that crate, but one thing we do know is that it was something important enough to have a foreign sub, likely Russian, bring it to our shore and transfer it along with one person to that fishing boat. It was then taken to Portland, unloaded into a van, and the crate and one person drove off. That's what we know.

Frankly, I'm betting that what you just saw was the transfer of a nuclear warhead onto U.S. soil. The fact that a foreign sub was involved makes it highly unlikely that it was a drug deal....they just don't merit war machines. What are your thoughts?"

Josh Dillon said, "I agree, I think we just witnessed the nuclear warhead for Project BS come ashore."

Sam Back nodded affirmatively and said, "Undoubtedly, That's the only thing that would make sense. Sadly, it took place 4 months ago. There's certainly no doubt the thing is in place to use by now. I guess the really good news is that we know the fishing boat that transported the person and crate from the sub. We can now get the names of the Captain and crew and do whatever's necessary to extract information from them. Maybe they'll even cooperate."

President DeVore replied, "Yeah, I know the CIA guys are on it as we speak. And I'm betting that there are security cameras around that Portland Marina parking lot, and I think we will be able get our hands on the data from those cameras to see if we can get a license number or any other identification on the van. We might get lucky there. Any other thoughts?"

Rudy Lester said, "Some of our personnel are on their way to Portland as we speak. They'll do everything possible to interview the boat's captain and crew and expedite getting that camera data and scanning it to identify the van. Keep your fingers crossed."

"Good. Let's hope and pray this is the break we so desperately need. Just as soon as I hear back from Rudy that he's got something I'll either call another meeting or we'll just handle it with a conference call. At any rate, I'll keep you posted. Thanks again for all your efforts. Our meeting is adjourned." All stood as the President exited the room.

Chapter 15

Present Time

November 1

City of Cumberland, Harlan County, Kentucky

It was 3:30 on Friday afternoon. Sheriff Sterling was holding the weekly meeting at the Harlan County Sheriff's Department's satellite office in Cumberland. Agents Cody Short and Sammy King were with him. His five deputies that operated out of the Cumberland office as well as Deputy Kyle Potter from the Harlan office were seated alongside Short and King. Bert stood before the group and said, "Okay guys, I got 3:30 and I think everyone's here so lets get started." First the sheriff asked Deputy Potter to report on the new Geiger Counters that had been ordered and should be received within the next few days. Deputy Potter explained that they had reason to believe that some of the rocket material might be radioactive, and that the Geiger Counters should be used to snoop around anything suspicious. He told the deputies to explain to anyone watching that the devices 'sniffed for drugs'. He said he would distribute them as soon as they arrived, likely early next week.

The sheriff then said, "Thanks Kyle. We do need to be very careful not to alarm anyone with the use of the Geiger Counters. We should continue to use the drug story to cover our searches and to say the Counters are 'drug sniffers'. Also as Kyle mentioned, aircraft will be back in the air over the county looking for anything suspicious. Again, if anyone questions them just say they are looking for the drug shipment. Other than that, unless someone has discovered something they want to report we'll call it a day."

Agent Sammy King held up his hand. Bert nodded to him, and the agent said, "As you all know, Agent Short and I have been searching along the county's main roads. I started where highway 421 crosses into Virginia going toward Pennington Gap and worked my way back to Harlan. Agent Short started where highway 38 crosses the Virginia line and worked his way back to Evarts and then to Harlan. The two of us then worked highway 119 from

Harlan to here in Cumberland. Tomorrow Agent Short will continue from Cumberland on highway 119 to the Letcher County line. I'll be going from Cumberland to the top of Black Mountain on highway 160. I thought we should let you know we'll be working in your area."

Bert said, "Thanks Sammy. That's good information for the other deputies here to know. Anything else?"

No one raised a hand or said anything. The five deputies from the Cumberland office left the meeting. The two agents, Deputy Potter and the sheriff remained in the meeting room.

Agent Short said, "Guys, I was called by Director Lester last night and was told that the agency had discovered what they believed to be the transfer of the rocket's warhead into the U.S. Apparently it was done by water off the coast of Maine and then transported by a black van presumably to Harlan County. I know that Agent King and I had not told you that we believe the warhead is nuclear, but we do believe that to be the case. You were correct to get those Geiger Counters. They could certainly turn up something. The agency is currently trying to find out additional information to pinpoint who got the warhead and where it was taken. I'll keep you posted."

Agent King then said, "You guys have a safe trip back to Harlan. Cody and I are staying at a motel here in

Cumberland tonight, and will get an early start tomorrow on our searches."

The four men shook hands and then departed.

• • •

Present Time, Next Day
November 2
CIA headquarters, Langley, Virginia

CIA Director Rudy Lester sat at the head of the table in a conference room. Three other CIA personnel were in attendance. Agents Forester, Moses, and Squibb.

The director said, "From what I understand we haven't been successful in our attempts to identify the fishing boat captain and crew or the van and driver. Please tell me the details." He then looked directly at Agent Moses.

Moses said, "I was assigned to check out the fishing boat and crew. It turned out to be an easy job. Two days after the alleged transfer took place the headlines of the Portland newspaper read 'Fishing boat and crew lost at sea'. As it turns out, the day after arriving back in port and transferring the man and warhead to the van the fishing boat, the Eleanor G, went back to sea. Late that afternoon another fishing boat happened upon what appeared to be the remains of the Eleanor G. The Coast Guard was called. After gathering all the floating remains from the boat they declared that an explosion had occurred, likely killing everyone on board. No human remains were ever found. End of story."

The director nodded, shook his head, and then looked at Agent Squibb, who said, "Agent Forester and I were assigned the job of getting any security camera data that was available for the time that the van was spotted in the parking lot. There were several security cameras in operation, but after viewing the data from them we were not able to get a shot of the license plate. We only know that it was a late model black Chevy suburban van. That's it."

Again, the director nodded and said, "Thanks guys. I'm sorry you weren't able to identify the bad guy and his crated package, but it's not your fault. You did all you could. I think the next step will be a tough one, but we've got to now (1) take a look at data from any security cameras along the major routes out of Portland. We just might get lucky and one of them have the back of the van with its license plate. And (2) we've got to check out all the rental companies to see if any rented a black Chevy Suburban van around the time in question. And I know these will take some time. And we certainly don't have a lot of it left. You three get started and request any additional personnel you need. Our country's security is at stake. Get back with me as soon as you learn anything."

• • •

Later that same day
BSC site
Black Mountain, Kentucky

It was late on Saturday afternoon. Bennie worked Monday through Friday. The contractors had just finally finished the columns this past Thursday. Ralph and Max were sitting at their desks.

Ralph said, "Max, I don't know about you, but I feel like a kid around the first of December wishing Christmas would hurry up and get here. I think we're now in pretty good shape. The columns are all finished and we've got the rocket all stowed and ready to go. The Elliott boom truck rental got delivered yesterday, and here we sit. But we got 25 more days to go before we light up that rocket. I'm anxious!"

"Yeah, I hear you," Max replied. "I feel the same way. I'm really anxious to get back home, and I know you're anxious to head west and buy that ranch. Unfortunately, we gotta sit here and mind the store until the 27th. But we are being well paid!"

Ralph smiled and said, "Yes we are, and that's what makes it bearable. I guess we just daydream about November 28th, Thanksgiving. It sure takes on a new meaning this year."

• • •

Ralph looked at Max and said, "My friend, it's almost 5:30. Why don't we call it a day?

Max glanced at the monitors and replied, "It looks like we got a visitor."

Both men watched as FBI Special Agent Sammy King parked his black sedan and walked toward the office building.

"That guy looks like trouble to me," Max said.

"We'll see," replied Ralph.

There was a knock on the door. Ralph walked to it, opened it, and said, "Yes sir, may I help you?"

Agent King flashed his government badge and said, "I'm FBI Special Agent Sammy King. I just wanted to ask you a few questions. May I come in."

"Sure," Ralph replied. "But you're working a tad late aren't you?"

The agent said, "Well, I guess so, but you're at the end of the road up here....my last call today."

"This is my associate Mr. Max Baker," Ralph said.

Agent King and Max shook hands. Max then said, "Pleased to meet you."

Ralph said, "Please have a seat. What exactly can we do for you Agent King?"

All three sat.

Agent King said, "My call is just a routine one. We have reason to believe that a large shipment of drugs recently came into Harlan County. All of Sheriff Sterling's deputies and one other agent and myself are searching the county looking for these drugs. As I said, your location is the very last one on highway 160....so you're the end of the line for me today. No one is accused of harboring drugs. We think the bad guys may well have hidden the large shipment somewhere on private property, perhaps even totally unknown to the property owner. So we're just going to homes and businesses and taking a quick look around to see if we might locate the drugs. We think they could well be hidden without the owner's knowledge."

"I see," Ralph said. "So what can we do for you?"

The agent said, "Well, with your permission I'd just

like to take a look around your operation. We could start here in the office building and then go outside, if that's okay?"

"Certainly," Ralph and Max replied in unison. All three stood. Agent King began walking around the office. He opened and looked in the restroom, and then in the storage room. He smiled and said, "Well, that didn't take long. Could we go outside and take a look around?"

"Absolutely," replied Rallph.

All three walked out the door. Agent King walked toward the columns and said, "My, my, those columns are tall. How tall are they?"

"30 feet," replied Max.

"And what are they for?" asked Sammy.

Ralph said, "They will support the platform that will in turn support the large antenna that we will be constructing here. The contractors just finished the columns this week. We're now in a hold mode until the contractors for the platform can get here and get underway with it. They should be here next week, but with contractors you just never know."

"I understand," Agent King replied. He then walked around all the columns and then returned beside Max and Ralph and said, "Okay, all this looks good." He then pointed toward the storage building and said, "I think that building over there is about all that's left. Could I take a look in it?"

"With all due respect, Agent King, everything in that building is highly confidential. It requires a top secret security clearance," replied Ralph.

Agent King pulled out his credentials wallet, flipped it open, and pointed to the words:
Security Clearance - Top Secret. He said, "That good enough?"

Ralph and Max looked at each other and shrugged. Ralph then said, "That's as good as it gets."

They walked to the storage building. Max entered the code for the overhead door. It opened and the three walked in.

The agent looked at the pieces of pipe and said, "Top Secret required for pipe?"

"No, it's what everything in here will be used for," replied Ralph. "That pipe and the electronic gear in the boxes will be used to construct some very confidential parts that will be assembled on the antenna. And I'm sorry, but that's about all I can say about it."

"No problem," Sammy replied. "Would it be a problem to open the boxes and have a look?"

Ralph said, "No. We can do that." He then pulled a pocket knife and sliced through the tape on the top of all four boxes. He then folded the cardboard flaps back to expose the smaller boxes inside.

Agent King walked up to one of the large boxes and reached in and pulled out two of the smaller ones. "Could I look in these?" he asked.

Ralph cut the tape and opened the two small boxes. Each contained electronic components that were originally on an outdated computer system. The agent took each of them, looked closely at them, and said, "Okay." He then put his hand into the large box and stirred around all the small boxes in it. He then walked over to another of the large boxes and pulled out one small box and said, "Could we look in this one?" Ralph cut the tape on the box. Agent King looked inside and extracted the part. It looked like a large relay switch. He put it back in the box and said, "That's good." He then walked to the two large boxes that he had not yet looked into and reached inside each, running his hand to the bottom.

Sammy then said, "Okay guys, that's good enough. No drugs here. I really thank you for being so cooperative and helpful. I'm sorry I had to cause you this trouble. It's just that we suspect the drugs are somewhere hidden in an unlikely spot."

Ralph replied, "We understand, Agent King. No problem at all. Glad to be of help."

The three walked back outside and Max hit the button to close the door.

As they walked back to Agent King's car Ralph said, "You be careful driving back off this mountain. That road's really curvy."

"Yeah, I noticed that coming up," Sammy said. "And I bet it's just as curvy going down!"

All shook hands, and Sammy got in his car, turned it around, and drove off.

Ralph looked at Max and said, "Max, you didn't even break a sweat!"

"But I'm sure glad he didn't check my blood pressure and heart rate," Max replied.

Ralph said, "Ha Ha Ha I understand....I felt the same way. It isn't every day an FBI agent calls. But I think the visit went well. We're just fortunate we put that cover equipment in there. We'd have been dead in the water if we hadn't."

"I'm going to sleep well tonight, Max."

The two locked up the office building, got in their cars, and headed for the Benham Hotel.

Chapter 16

Present Time

November 4

Wallops Island, Virginia

The director of the Glider and Rocket Museum at Wallops Island, Mr. Frank Schrodt, had called a meeting with his three museum board members, Willie Reucroft, Lee Kon, and Eric Eaton. They were convened after work in a Wallops Island conference room.

Director Schrodt said, "Guys I called this meeting for a couple of reasons. First, I doubt that you are aware of it, but a few weeks ago the NASA bosses here at Wallops got a request from the CIA to check the inventory of all rockets capable of launching a payload of 400 pounds or more. Apparently the CIA had reason to believe that such a rocket might be missing from our inventory. I understand the directive was sent to all locations inventorying such rockets. A memo went out to several bosses here at Wallops and our inventory was all accounted for and so reported back to the CIA. I did not receive the directive, but just yesterday was talking with my boss and he mentioned the inventory search that was made. It occurred to me during our conversation that the Aerobee 170A that we have in our museum is capable of launching a 500 pound payload, and I told my boss. He sort of laughed, but then asked that I verify that we still had it. I told him I certainly thought we did, and that it was stored at Ralph Keelen's farm, awaiting our finding a new location for the museum. So, we do need to verify that it is there. The second thing I wanted to tell you is that we have completed working out a lease from a farmer only about 5 miles from the base that will let us occupy one of his buildings for our museum. The building is very close to the highway, and is in super good shape. The building was previously leased to a tractor sales company but their lease ran out and they elected to locate elsewhere. The only thing we need to do to it is to modify the roof in one section so that we can exhibit the Aerobee in its vertical position. I've already met with a contractor that says he can do that modification within our present budget, and that it should be completed within 90 days. So we need to start moving both our glider planes and rockets to the new location. It has loads of floor space. I know it's going to be a lot of trouble to move the gliders, we'll have to remove their wings to transport them, and it'll be a pain to move all the rockets from the Keelen farm, but we gotta do it."

Lee Kon held up his hand. Schrodt acknowledged him. Lee said, "Frank, I've got the key to Ralph Keelen's barn where the rockets are all stored, so we could verify the Aerobee and then move all the rockets whenever you wish. We'll just need to borrow some trucks from the base to move them."

Frank Schrodt said, "Yeah, and I think we should do that as soon as possible. My boss would like the Aerobee verification asap, and we need to get the rockets moved in before we start relocating the glider planes. Borrowing trucks to move the rockets will not be a problem. What do you think about the four of us asking off Wednesday afternoon for making the rocket move? It shouldn't take more than 5 or 6 hours."

The three museum board members nodded their heads affirmatively. Lee Kon said, "I'll pick up one truck and meet you guys at the Keelen farm around 1 pm on Wednesday, that be okay?"

Frank Schrodt said, "Sounds good to me. I'll pick up another truck. I think two will be plenty. Eric and Willie, can you meet us there?"

"Sure," Eric and Willie said in unison.

"Great," Frank Schrodt said. "Meeting adjourned."

• • •

Earlier That Same Day
CIA Headquarters
Langley, Virginia

Director Lester once again sat at the conference table, along with Agents Forester, Moses, and Squibb. The director said, "Hey guys, I really appreciate the quick work. Only two days and we meet again. I understand you have had some good luck."

Agent Forester replied, "Yes and no, Director Lester. We were able to identify the black van both from several security cameras along the route it took out of town, and also found the company that rented the van. We got the license number from the security camera data, and it corresponded to the van rental. But that's about as far as we got, unfortunately. Apparently the van was rented using a stolen credit card and fake driver's license in the same name. So that didn't help us ID the driver. But we did confirm that the van was dropped off at a rental location in downtown Harlan, Kentucky. Unfortunately it was left after hours, and the lot where it was parked did not have security cameras. We even checked other security cameras around town, but had no luck. So all we really have is that the driver and its crated box went to Harlan County. Maybe that will be of some help."

Director Lester nodded, rubbed his chin, and said, "That was good work. It sure would have been great if we could have identified the driver, but you did all you could. At least it does confirm that the person and crated box are likely somewhere in Harlan County. I'll pass that information along."

• • •

Two Days Later
November 6
Chincoteague, Virginia

.

It was 12:30 pm. Lee Kon had arrived driving a Wallops Island truck to the Keelen farm 30 minutes before the scheduled meeting at 1 pm. Lee wanted to check to make sure everything looked good with the fake Aerobee.

He carefully looked it over from payload to engine and found everything in order. He then sat and started to think about the arrangement he had with Ralph Keelen. The farm was appraised at about $250,000. Lee had told Ralph that he really liked the farm and would love to buy it, but he didn't think he would be able to afford it. Ralph gave it some thought and then told Lee that he would sell it to him for $125,000, half the appraised value. He told him he could write a postdated check dated the first day of next year, and by that time he should be able to set up financing for the farm and Ralph would be settled somewhere out west and back using his real identity. Lee jumped at the opportunity. He was sure he'd be able to put together the down payment for the mortgage based on a selling price of only $125,000, half the appraised value. So he had given Ralph his post dated check, and Ralph had signed over the deed to him, dated the first of the year. Lee couldn't wait to move to the farm.

"Hey guy....wake up," Frank Schrodt shouted to Lee. "We got work to do."

Lee snapped out of his daydream and said, "Oh, hi Frank. "Yeah, I'm ready."

Eric Eaton and Willie Reucroft walked into the barn behind Frank. Eric said, "The gang's all here....let's get these rockets loaded!"

Lee said, "If I might make a suggestion, I'm familiar with the Aerobee. Why don't I break it down into it's segments and load it with the fork lift, and you guys work on getting all the smaller rockets loaded. That be okay?"

Frank said, "Sounds like a plan to me. Let's make it happen."

Lee started to dismantle the fake Aerobee, and the other three began to move all the other rockets into Frank's truck.

The Aerobee was horizontal in a wooden cradle that had been made for the purpose. Lee carefully disassembled the four segments, and then using the forklift carefully placed each into his truck. He then loaded the cradle, and was all set to truck it to the new museum site. The other three guys had finished loading all the other rockets and were sitting enjoying soft drinks that Frank had provided from a cooler he brought.

Lee said, "Okay, I got the Aerobee all secured, and it looks like you guys got everything else. After I wolf down one of those drinks we'll be all ready to roll to our new museum."

Frank threw Lee a cold soda and said, "Bottom's up, we need to hit the road so we can get everything unloaded before dark. Incidentally, since we found the Aerobee okay I'll report back to my boss that it's accounted for. Lee, do you know how to get to the new museum?"

Lee nodded affirmatively with a grin. He said, "Sure do. It's sorta hard to get lost on Wallops Island!"

After finishing their refreshments the four departed the Keelen farm for the new museum site.

• • •

Same Day
three hours later
Wallops Island, Virginia

"Ahh, the ole sun is setting, but we've accomplished our mission. All the rockets are unloaded in their new home!," Frank Schrodt proclaimed.

The four were now sitting outside the new museum on the tailgate of Eric Eaton's pickup truck. They were finishing off the drinks in Frank's cooler and had just locked up the museum, and would head home just as soon as they finished their brief rest.

Inside the museum the Aerobee had been reassembled by Lee with the help of a forklift that the farmer who owned the building had loaned them. Lee had carefully reassembled all the four segments and then positioned the rocket back on the wooden cradle in the horizontal position. Unknown to him, however, was the fact that a large nail in the cradle had gotten dislodged during the move, and when he laid the assembled rocket down into the cradle the nail punctured the skin on the rocket sustainer section. No one noticed the puncture, but a stream of sand was now pouring from the sustainer to the floor beneath it.

Frank said, "Well guys, thanks so much for your help. The next step will be to move the gliders to the museum, but we've got to wait until week-end after next before doing that. I couldn't line up all the glider owners before then. Once we get them in, and get the roof construction finished for the Aerobee, we'll be able to start putting up new signage and sprucing up the place for an opening. I'll keep you posted. Again, thanks for all the help."

All four slapped each other on the back, shook hands, and got in their vehicles to head home.

Chapter 17

Present Time
November 9
Harlan, Kentucky

Sheriff Sterling, Deputy Potter, and Agents Cody Short and Sammy King had just finished lunch at El Charrito's Mexican restaurant in the Village Center Mall just outside Harlan. All four had ordered the delicious chicken soup, upon the recommendation of Kyle Potter.

Deputy Potter said, "Well guys, was my recommendation on target?"

Sammy King said, "Was it ever. That's the best chicken soup I ever had. It's certainly different from what I'm used to."

Bert and Cody nodded agreement. Cody said, "I'll ditto that. I didn't know chicken soup could be so good!"

Bert looked at his watch and said, "We've only got about a half hour before Director Lester is scheduled to arrive. I think we should be moving."

All agreed, stood, paid the cashier, and walked to Bert's cruiser.

They drove the short distance to the Appalachian Regional Hospital, which was clearly visible from the restaurant, less than a quarter mile away. CIA Director Rudy Lester was to arrive via helicopter at the hospital helipad at 1 pm. The hospital administrator had gladly arranged for a conference room to be available to the group. To the casual observer, the helicopter would just be one of many delivering patients daily to the hospital. And that's exactly what was wanted. A visit to Harlan County by the Director of the Central Intelligence Agency would be top news and raise all kinds of questions. And that was not wanted.

The group met Mayor Fred Knapp as they arrived at the hospital parking lot. The mayor couldn't join them for lunch due to another commitment but wanted to attend the meeting with Director Lester. As they all walked toward the hospital entrance Fred said, "I bet you boys are full of chicken soup!"

Bert smiled and said, "Now Fred, how did you guess that?"

Fred replied, "I've gone there with Kyle many times. He always gets the soup and persuades me to do the same. And I'm always glad I did!. That's good stuff."

Kyle grinned and the two agents nodded vigorously.

They entered the hospital and went up to the heliport on the roof. After doing the chit-chat for a few minutes they suddenly heard the sound of a helicopter approaching. All stepped back toward the roof door to maintain a safe distance from the aircraft. It sat down, and after the rotors stopped Director Lester jumped out. He rushed over to the awaiting group, greeted everyone, and suggested they proceed to the conference room, which they did.

Mayor Knapp was the first to speak after everyone had a seat. "Director Lester, on behalf of the good people of Harlan I want to welcome you. It certainly isn't very often we get visits from such high ranking officials. I wish we could have announced your visit, in which case you'd have had a tremendous welcome, but I understand the circumstances and just want to say that we'll certainly continue to cooperate any way you wish. Welcome to Harlan."

Rudy Lester replied, "Why thank you Mayor Knapp. I appreciate your warm comments. And I truly do wish my visit here was for pleasure, or at least of a non-confidential nature, but sadly that's not the case. So, let's get to our business, which is, as you know, Project BS. Today marks 18 days until the Thanksgiving holiday begins. We've been working on this now for just over a month. I'm not here to criticize anyone, or to negatively reflect on your efforts. In fact, from what I hear from Agents King and Short you're doing an outstanding job. But the bottom line is that with just a little over two weeks to go we don't know who the bad guys are or where they've hidden that rocket. Of course there's always a slight chance that it's not even here in Harlan County, and if that's the case then Lord be with us. But we still have every reason to think it's here somewhere. I think we're working with some pretty sophisticated bad guys. We've just got to do something to fish them out."

He then took a sip of water, and continued, "Let me briefly review what we've been doing on a federal level. Firstly, we were successful searching our satellite data to locate the transfer of what we believe to have been the warhead from a submarine, likely Soviet, to a fishing boat off the coast of Maine. We tracked the fishing boat to a marina in Portland, and then saw one person and his crated box transferred to a black van in the marina parking lot. We were able to trace the van to its rental agency, but unfortunately a stolen credit card and false driver's license were used and we were unable to ID the driver. The van was checked-in at a rental location in downtown Harlan, but it was dropped off after hours and there were no surveillance cameras to capture the driver. So really all we know about this is that the one person and the mysterious box are likely somewhere in the county."

He took another sip of water and said, "And finally, we did a very thorough search of our entire rocket inventory and have not been able to identify any missing rocket capable of lifting a 400 pounds or more payload. So we've struck out here also. Agents Short and King tell me that county aerial surveillance using planes and helicopters has not produced anything suspicious. So, that's about where we stand. Is there anything new on your end that you could share with me?"

Deputy Potter held up his hand. Director Lester looked at him and nodded. Kyle said, "Mr. Director, we did just a couple of days ago get in a shipment of Geiger Counters, and these have now been distributed to all the deputies and your agents. Our hope is that they may detect something radioactive that could identify the rocket. Everyone using one has been told to explain them to outsiders as drug sniffers."

"And that was an excellent idea, Deputy Potter," Rudy Lester said. "Let's hope they pay off. Anyone else have anything they'd like to share, including any ideas to consider?"

Sheriff Sterling said, "Director, as you said, we've been going about the search now for a little more than a month, and we simply haven't found anything suspicious. My Deputy Rosie Cain has been pouring over the court records looking for anything there that might indicate suspicious activity. But thus far, nothing. As you pointed out, these people, if in our county, are very professional and have kept the rocket and warhead well hidden. I really don't have any suggestions for doing anything differently. As far as I'm concerned, we just have to keep up the search and hope something turns up. We all realize how important it is, and all my deputies are working well over regular hours to accomplish their responsibilities. I still feel that if it's in Harlan County we'll find it.'

Agent Sammy King then raised his hand. "Yes Sammy, speak," Rudy said.

"Thanks, Rudy," Agent King replied. "I haven't said anything about this to anyone up to now, but one week ago today I searched a site on Black Mountain called BSC. They stated that they are in the process of constructing a huge antenna that will receive and transmit confidential data for the government. Currently they have four huge concrete columns completed, and said they are ready to construct a platform on the columns that will support the antenna. I searched their office, the site around the construction, and then looked in a storage building that they said contained very confidential parts and equipment. They required me to show my Top Secret credentials in order to look in the building. Inside there were several pieces of long pipe and four sealed boxes of what they described as electronic gear to be assembled along with the pipe on the antenna. And they said they really couldn't discuss that any further. I checked out the boxes and sure enough they did contain electronic parts. But something there just didn't smell exactly right to me. And I'm still not sure what it was. I've been thinking about it for the past week, and still I'm not sure why, but something there just didn't seem to add up. Maybe I shouldn't have brought it up, but that's about the only thing I've seen that might even be considered slightly suspicious, but I really don't have a reason to think that. Any thoughts from you other guys?"

Sheriff Sterling spoke up, "Sammy, thanks for those comments. I did visit the site also. They hired a person named Bennie Sekao that in times past was considered the Harlan town drunk. I've known Bennie many years, and have had to arrest him almost weekly for being publicly drunk. But since BSC hired him he's turned his life around. He's quit drinking and he's made them a very reliable employee. They praised him highly. So I actually went primarily as a social call, but I was also interested in their operation. A lot of people in Harlan County have been talking about it, and speculating on its nature. So I drove there one afternoon and visited. There were three in the office when I was there. Bennie, a Mr. Ralph Neleek, and a Mr. Max Baker. Neleek seemed to be the head guy. Baker said very little, but when he did speak I noticed a pretty heavy accent. He said he was originally from Italy. But the thing that struck me was that during my days in the navy I was stationed for about six months in Naples. I heard a lot of Italian accent, but none seemed to sound like Max. I didn't really think much of it at the time, but it did strike me as strange. Other than that, everything seemed above board with their operation as far as I could tell. So I couldn't add much to explain Sammy's concerns."

Sammy said, "Thanks sheriff, I do remember that Max was quiet, but when he did speak I too noticed the accent. But I didn't pay enough attention to it to say what kind of accent it might have been."

Director Lester then said, "Well, unless anyone has something else, I think we've accomplished what I came here for. I suggest you guys keep at the search, and I hope those Geiger Counters turn up something. We'll continue to work on it from our end, but I'm not real hopeful there. I might suggest that since the Black Mountain Site seemed to perhaps be a bit suspicious, you might want to make a return visit there under some pretense and do a little more questioning and snooping. One thing I can do from my end is check this BSC company out. I'll keep you posted on what I learn. Is that it?"

Mayor Knapp said, "Director Lester, thank you for visiting with us. I feel this whole thing will get resolved soon. I know how important it is, and I have every confidence in the people working on it. If you would permit me, could I share a story I heard yesterday?

Everyone in the room grinned except Rudy Lester, who said, "By all means, Mr. Mayor."

Fred began, "Well, it seems there was this new army base just opening up. A very pompous Major had been assigned an office on the base and was getting all his stuff moved in. The Major, who had an exceedingly high opinion of himself, was always trying to impress those around him. One day a private knocked on his office door. In order to impress whomever was knocking on the door the Major picked up his desk phone, put it to his ear, and shouted to the knocker, 'Come on in'. The private entered the office and head the Major speak into his phone saying,

'Yes General, I'll take care of it immediately,'. and then hangs up. Feeling he had impressed the private sufficiently he then said, 'Yes private...what do you want?' To which the private said, "Nothing really important, sir, I'm just here to connect your telephone!'"

Rudy Lester and the other four roared with laughter. The Director then said, "I'll remember that one and tell it to some of my army buddies. I have several in mind that could pass for that major!'"

The conference room emptied as the group headed upstairs to the heliport to see Director Lester off.

Chapter 18

Present Time

November 16

Harlan, Kentucky

Sheriff Sterling and Mayor Knapp were huddled together at a table in Creech Cafe at mid morning. Fred said, "Bert, a week has passed since Director Lester's Harlan visit and we still don't have anything new on Project BS?"

"I'm afraid that's the case," Bert replied. "And frankly, we're not too far from having completing the search. As a matter of fact, Agents Short and King have finished their assigned areas. But still nothing."

"Well, we got 11 days before the Thanksgiving holiday. We need to remain positive," Fred said.

Bert replied, "You know Fred, I'm considering going over to Maggard's Grocery and having a little man to man talk with Trigger Green. He knows everything illegal going on in the county, and although he's always out to make a dollar without regard for the law, he does have a good heart and certainly wouldn't want a disaster like the rocket shot to happen. He might know something and be willing to share. What do you think about running Project BS by him?"

Fred thought for a minute and said, "It would be a bit chancy, but given the fact that we're running out of time maybe it would be a good move. Like you, I think Trigger would keep it quiet and if he did know something I think he'd likely share it once he realized the magnitude of the looming disaster. I'd say go for it."

"You don't think we need approval from the G-men?" asked Bert.

"No," replied the Mayor. "I think if you asked them they'd just say they had to ask their bosses in Washington, and that could take months. We don't have the time."

Bert said, "Okay, I feel you're right. I think I'll head over to Maggards for a visit."

The sheriff then stood to leave, but noticed a recent posting on the wall beside him. He said, "This a new one Fred?"

The mayor said with a smile, "It is."

Bert starting reading the article:

A young lady brought her fiancé home to meet her parents. After dinner, the mother asked her husband to find out about the young man. The father asked the fiancé to join him in his study for a chat. He said, "So, what are your plans?"

The young man replied, "I am a biblical scholar."

The father responded, "Admirable, but how will you provide a nice house for my daughter to live in?"

"I will study," said the young man, "and God will provide."

"And how will you buy her a beautiful engagement ring, as she deserves?" the father asked.

"I will concentrate on my studies, and God will provide for us," he replied.

"What about children?' asked the father.

"No worry....God will provide for us," the fiancé said.

After several more minutes of questions with the fiancé always answering the same, "God will provide for us," the father ended the chat.

Later the mother asked the father, "Well, how did your talk with him go?"

The father said, "I learned he's a Democrat. He has no job. He has no plans, and he thinks I'm God!"

Bert left Creech Cafe with a smile on his face.

. . .

Same Day

Wallops Island, Virginia

Frank Schrodt yelled at one of the glider owners, "Be careful....watch the plane's tail when you swing her around. It's going to be close to the wall."

The owners of the gliders in the museum were moving their planes into position. Everything had gone smoothly. Only one more glider to bring in. Frank started walking back toward the entrance door. As he passed the Aerobee rocket lying in its cradle he glanced down and saw the large pile of what appeared to be sand under the front sustainer section. He walked over to it, squatted down, looked closely, and gathered a handfull. It was sand. He then saw the large nail sticking in the ragged tare in the rocket's body. He felt of the tare, and realized the body was made of wood. Certainly not the material required for a rocket. He stood up with a very puzzled look on his face. He then pulled out his pocket knife and walked back to the booster stage. He stabbed the knife into the side of the booster. Sand started pouring out, and again he found the booster material to be wooden.

"Hey Frank, can we move my glider in now?" asked the owner of the last glider.

"It's gonna have to wait a few minutes.....I gotta call my boss."

. . .

Later That Day
Harlan County, Kentucky

Fatso jumped awake from his nap when he heard the doorbell jingle. He looked toward the door and said, "I do believe we're honored by the presence of Harlan County Sheriff J. Bert Sterling.'

Bert walked over to the check-out counter and said, "Fatso, you're looking good. I was hoping that I might have a few words with Trigger. Is he in?"

"I think that could be arranged," Fatso replied. "But first, tell me why couldn't two elephants go swimming together?"

Bert grinned and said, "Cause they'd sink?"

Fatso smiled, shook his head, and said, "Because they only had one pair of trunks!"

"I guess that makes sense," the sheriff replied. "Now, can I go see Trigger?"

"I'm pushing the button as we speak. His door is unlocked. You go right ahead, I'm sure he'll be pleased to see you."

"Come in, come in," shouted Trigger upon hearing the knock on his door.

"Hey Bert, so good to see you.....I hope," Trigger said as he stood and shook hands with the sheriff. "Please do come in and have a seat. A social call, I hope."

Bert smiled and said, "I wish. No, I've got some really important information I want to share with you. And I'd sure appreciate it if you would agree to keep what I'm about to tell you confidential. If word got out it could potentially be really bad."

Trigger frowned and said, "Sounds serious, Bert. Sure, I'll keep it quiet."

Bert then told Trigger about the suspected rocket being in Harlan County, and asked if he might be able to shed any light on it."

Trigger said, "I've sure heard about the large drug shipment that you and your deputies were searching for. Now I understand why it was something I was not aware of. I'm normally in the loop on anything like a large drug shipment into the county."

Trigger thought for a minute and said, "Bert, I just don't know anything about a rocket. But I will think about it, and do a little snooping to see if I can turn up anything. The last thing in the world I'd want is for a disaster like that to occur in our county. Not only could a lot of people be harmed, but it would also be bad for my business!"

"It would," Bert replied with a grin. "Okay Trigger, that was what I wanted to share with you, and again, please keep it under wraps."

"Will do," Trigger said as he stood and shook the sheriff's hand. "Tell Rosie, Kyle and Mayor Knapp hello for me."

The sheriff nodded as he turned and left Trigger's office. As he was approaching the front door he heard Fatso yell, "Hey Bert, What is big, grey, and has a lot of red bumps?"

Bert continued to walk toward the door.

Fatso shouted, "An elephant that was stung by a lot of bees!"

The doorbell tingled as the sheriff walked out shaking his head.

• • •

Same Time
CIA Headquarters
Langley, Virginia

Director Rudy Lester sat at his desk. He had just received a phone call from the NASA Administrator at Wallops Island telling him the news about the Aerobee rocket in the museum there. Rudy had a very worried look on his face. He picked up his phone and dialed Agent Cody Short.

"Cody, this is Rudy Lester. I just received a call from Wallops Island telling me that the Aerobee rocket they have in their museum is a fake. It looked identical to the real thing, but the skin got punctured and sand fell out. And it was discovered to be made of wood. It was a super replica, but a fake. So my guess is that we now know that the rocket there in Harlan County is an Aerobee 170A, and it is fully capable of launching a 500 pound payload."

A stunned Agent Short replied, "Wow! That is news! Do we know anything about how the switch was made, and who might have transported the rocket here?"

"Not yet," the Director said, "but we're sure working on it. We feel for the first time that we have a real good lead. I just wanted to call to let you know. But until we uncover additional information about the person responsible for the switch we can only confirm the type of rocket. And the characteristics of that Aerobee correspond to the physical size and weight you already had. So right now nothing new that can really help you, but hopefully very soon we'll be able to identify the person responsible and have something new for you. Listen for my call!"

"Will I ever," said Cody Short. "Thanks for the heads up, Mr. Director."

• • •

Same Time
Harlan County, Kentucky

Trigger Green was very concerned about the information the sheriff had just passed to him. He sat at his desk and thought about everything he was presently involved with in the county, and that was quite a bit. As he thought about things over the past year that could have related to the rocket the only thing that stood out in his mind was the BSC operation at Black Mountain. He recalled Mr. Neleek showed up at his store driving a rental truck. And that truck could certainly have contained rocket segments. Bert had said the rocket was 40 feet tall when assembled, but could likely be divided up into segments. And Pretty Boy had called him with several requests, including the strange load of pipe and boxes of electronic junk, cars for two men at the BSC site and then for two more old cars to be delivered there next week. And Trigger had been responsible for locating the site and getting it leased and then the contractors for building the columns and for making arrangements for the two men to stay at the Benham Hotel. Trigger thought all that was just speculation about it having anything to do with a rocket, but he couldn't think of anything else he had been into that fit. He certainly didn't want to tell Bert about his activity with the BSC site unless he was absolutely sure it was related to the rocket. He decided to continue to think about it, and maybe to check a little further about what was going on up on Black Mountain.

Chapter 19

Present Time

November 20

Benham, Kentucky

Ralph and Max were sitting together at the Benham Hotel having breakfast. Ralph said, "One week from today and we'll be able to light up that rocket and then go our merry ways. I can hardly wait."

Max responded, "Yeah. It's actually almost here. But we've got a big job to do tonight. Do you think we're ready?"

Ralph looked around to make sure no one was within listening range and said, "I think so. Everything we need is all there. I really think we'll get her all vertical and ready to go in no more than two to three hours. But we sure gotta be very careful. One little mistake at this point could ruin the whole thing."

Max said, "Well, we got the boom truck all set and ready. Bennie will leave at 5, or certainly no later than 5:30. We have no contractors on site. Just as soon as it gets good and dark, around 6 pm, we should be able to get underway. The moon doesn't rise until around midnight, and then it's only a quarter moon. I feel certain we'll be finished with everything before the moon comes up. If we are able to get started around 6 pm, I believe by 10 we should be all wrapped up."

"I sure hope so," Ralph said. "Let's just go over everything one last time. After Bennie leaves I'll drive my car into the driveway, blocking any other cars from coming in. Someone could still walk in, but they'd need a flashlight, and we'd see it. We then open up the storage building and move the pipe and boxes outside, out of the way. We'll do that using the fork lift. Next we take down the false back wall. We should be able to do that in a half hour. Lot easier to take out than to put up. But we do need to be careful not to disturb any of the existing wall so that when the false wall is out it looks normal. We'll leave the brackets in place on the back wall and lay the pipe on them after we've gotten the rocket segments out. That wouldn't arouse any suspicion. We then move each rocket segment from its bracket to outside the building using the forklift. Next we assemble the rocket on the concrete pad in front of the storage building. The final segment to go into place will be the warhead. Max, you'll need to inspect it real good to make sure all the connections are made and that it looks good to go. I know you spent many nights working on it after it got here and before we hid it behind the fake wall, but this will be your last opportunity to check it. We then will attach the harness to the flange around the top of the sustainer stage and pull all the harness cables up into position beyond the warhead and attach them into the lifting ring. After this is done I'll bring the boom truck up and lower the boom such that we can pin the lifting ring into the end of the boom cable. Then I very, very slowly start to lift the rocket by raising the boom. The concrete column its going into is 30 feet high, and the rocket itself is 40 feet long, so I'll have to raise the end of the boom up to a little more than 70 feet. After I do this the rocket will be hanging vertically by the harness. At this point I will begin to move at a snail's pace over to the hollow concrete column. Once the tail of the rocket is directly centered over the column I'll start to lower it down using the boom's cable. This will be very critical. We must be certain that the rocket tail enters the column core without hitting the top of the column or rubbing on the core walls. Once it's started its descent into the core I'll very slowly lower it until it rests on the concrete pad at the bottom of the 10 foot hole under the column. At this point the rocket is in place. The tip of the warhead should be about a foot under the top of the column. I then press the button to release the boom cable from the lifting ring. When I do this the lifting ring will fall down onto the warhead and I can lower the boom cable down to the ground. You then attach the boom cable to the harness on the chair-lift. You have a seat in the chair and I lift you up until you're at the top of the column. You reach in, grab the rocket harness lifting ring, pull the pins from the cables that are attached to the flange on the top of the sustainer stage and pull those cables out. The rocket will then be ready to fire. I'll lower the man chair and the boom arm and we'll stow them both. I'll then go to the forklift and get the pipes and put them in the brackets on the back wall and then we'll move the four boxes of electronic junk back inside the storage building. All the wood that we removed from the fake back wall we'll have to put in our dumpster. We lock up the storage building and head back to the hotel. And hope that all goes well and we're back down the mountain and in bed well before midnight."

"You don't think there will be a chance a satellite will pick up our activity?" asked Max.

Ralph said, "Not if we don't use any flashlights. We'll wear our night vision goggles. We should be able to see everything with them. If we don't produce any light we won't be seen. Should go just fine."

Max nodded, "I'll sure feel lots better this time tomorrow morning."

"By then all we'll have left to do is put up with Bennie for another 6 days, light up the rocket, and then get out of Dodge," Ralph said.

Max said, "I'm not sure I know what getting out of Dodge means?"

Ralph laughed, took the last sip of his coffee, and said, "Don't worry....it just means we leave the scene."

The two stood up, walked to their cars, and started the drive up Black Mountain.

• • •

Later That Same Day
Harlan, Kentucky

Sheriff Sterling, sitting at his desk, heard the ring tone on his cell phone. He picked it up, punched a button, and said, "Sheriff Sterling here."

"Hi Bert, this is Rudy Lester. I just got off the phone with Agent Short giving him an update on our situation here. I wanted to share the same information with you."

"Thanks Rudy, I hope it's good news," Bert said.

"Well, sort of," the Director said. "A team of our agents picked up a fellow named Lee Kon that works as an electrician at Wallops Island. He was a close friend to the fellow that owned the farm where the museum rockets were temporarily stored for a while. That fellow's name is Ralph Keelen, although he goes by the nickname 'Geek'. Kon had the key to the barn where the rockets were all stored, and from what we've been able to find out the two were very knowledgeable about the rockets. Keelen is now missing. He resigned his position at Wallops Island saying he was moving west for health reasons. This happened a little more than 5 months ago. We don't know all the details, but what we've pieced together is that somehow Keelen was able to come up with a mock rocket that looked just like the Aerobee, and then it was filled with sand to give it weight similar to the rocket. He then switched the fake rocket for the Aerobee and headed for Kentucky. Fortunately for us, the museum director found a permanent location for the gliders and rockets, and when the fake Aerobee was moved it was damaged and discovered to be made of wood and filled with sand."

"Ahh," Bert replied. "Of course this Keelen would now be using a phony name and ID. Do you have a description of him?"

"Yep," Director Lester replied, "he's mid thirties, about average height and weight, and when last seen at Wallops Island had long hair tied into a pony tail and a full beard. He also wore thick glasses. I guess it was his appearance that gave him the nickname 'Geek'. Obviously he could have changed his appearance, but I'm 99% sure that the man we're looking for in Harlan County is Ralph 'Geek' Keelen."

"Well, that certainly gives us good information to go on," the sheriff said. "Did you get anything more from his buddy Lee Kon?"

"No, he's not been cooperating. We know that he originally came to the U.S. from North Korea, and was granted political asylum and the job at Wallops about 5 years ago. His record has been clean, but we now suspect he's a mole."

"If that's the case, you might not get anything else out of him," Bert said. "I think you're just really lucky that fake rocket got damaged. Now we've got something concrete to go on."

The director replied, "Yeah, that was my feeling as well."

Bert said, "Thanks so much for the info. I'll pass it along to my deputies, and we'll be digging on this end to locate Keelen. Please do keep me informed of anything new that develops there."

"Will do, sheriff," said Lester. "And good luck!"

•   •   •

Later That Same Day
BSC site
Black Mountain, Kentucky

Bennie looked at his watch and said, "Hey guys, I got 5:15. Time to call it a day. I think I'll head home and have dinner while I watch Jeopardy and Wheel of Fortune."

"Sounds exciting," Ralph said sarcastically. "I'm just kidding you, Bennie, you have a good evening."

Bennie said, "I'm sure going to try!" He stood, grabbed his jacket, and headed out the door.

Max and Ralph watched on the monitors until they saw his car was gone. Max then said, "That takes care of Bennie. Now we just wait a few minutes till it gets good and dark and we'll get that rocket all set."

Ralph nodded. The two went back to their computers.

•   •   •

45 Minutes Later

Ralph stood and said, "I'm going to move my car into the driveway."

Max stood and said, "Good. I'll go and open the storage building."

The two men exited the office building, locking the door behind them. Ralph positioned his car in the driveway such that it blocked any other car from entering, and then he walked to the storage building. The two men moved the boxes and pipes out beside the building using the forklift. They then went inside, shut the overhead door, turned on the lights and started walking toward the false back wall. Max said, "It's a good thing this building has no windows. Otherwise we'd have to be working in the dark."

Ralph laughed and nodded, then said, "Okay Max, lets attack that wall and get it down."

The two worked for about a half hour with crow bars and hammers and finally got all of the false back wall removed. All the pieces of wood and lumber were now piled beside the overhead door.

Ralph said, "Okay, time to put on the night vision glasses. But first, let me turn the lights in here off." Ralph turned out the lights as they both put on the glasses.

Max looked at Ralph and said, "You look a little green, but I can see you."

"Yeah," Ralph replied as he opened the overhead door. The two then piled all the wood from the fake back wall onto the forks of the forklift and Ralph drove it to the dumpster and disposed of it. They then began the process of moving the rocket segments to the concrete deck in front of the storage building. Ralph would drive the forklift and Max would assist loading and unloading and holding onto the rocket segments as they were moved. Finally they had all the segments moved. The two then moved the segments together and fastened them securely. They then looked at the assembled Aerobee 170A lying horizontally in front of the storage building.

Ralph said, "You satisfied with the warhead?"

"Yeah," Max replied. "I checked it out one last time. Everything seems fine. Let's get this thing vertical."

Max grabbed the rocket harness and secured it's cables to the top of the sustainer stage. He then pulled the cables up above the nose of the rocket and fastened them to the lifting ring. Ralph got on the boom truck and drove it to where when the boom was lowered it was close to the lifting ring. He then snapped the fastening pin at the end of the boom cable into the lifting ring.

Max then said, "She's ready to be lifted. Good luck!"

Ralph started raising the boom slowly and the cable at the end of the boom started to raise the rocket. After about 10 minutes the rocket reached the vertical position and lifted off the ground. Ralph continued to raise the boom until the bottom of the rocket looked to be a couple of feet above the top of the hollow concrete column. The tip of the warhead was now somewhere around 72 feet off the ground. Ralph then very gently moved the boom truck until the bottom of the rocket looked to be exactly above the centerline of the hollow column. He then started to inch it down. When the bottom of the rocket looked to be at about the top of the hollow column he slowed even more. Moving just millimeters at a time he lowered the rocket until it went into the core of the concrete column. He then sped up the descent and continued until the boom cable went slack, indicating that the rocket now rested on the concrete pad at the bottom of the 10 foot hole directly under the base of the column. He then punched the release button detaching the lifting ring from the boom cable. The lifting ring fell inside the column core, and Ralph lowered the boom cable to the ground.

He then looked at Max, grinned and said, "Okay Max, you ready for the ride up?"

Max gave Ralph a thumbs-up. He then grabbed the chair-lift and attached it's harness to the end of the boom cable. "Going up," he shouted.

Ralph started raising the boom cable. A couple of minutes later Max arrived at the top of the column. He leaned in and looked for the lifting ring, found it and removed the rocket harness cables from the sustainer flange. He stowed the lifting ring and cables and gave another thumbs-up to Ralph. The chair-lift then started its descent and was soon back on the ground.

Ralph jumped out of the boom truck cab. Ralph jumped out of the chair-lift. The two ran and embraced each other. Ralph said, "Man, we did it. We got us a live rocket ready to go. Let's get everything cleaned up around here and head for home."

The two then used the forklift to replace the boxes into the storage building and put the pipes on the back wall brackets. They then swept the floor before lowering the overhead door. Everything looked good.

Max looked at his watch. It was 10:30 pm. He said, "Not bad. Not bad at all! Let's get off this mountain."

Chapter 20

Present Time

November 22

Cumberland, Kentucky

Sheriff Sterling was holding the last weekly meeting at his satellite office in Cumberland. Agents Short and King were with him.

The sheriff said, "Okay guys, today is our last Project BS meeting. Unfortunately, so far our searches have been fruitless. And the Thanksgiving holidays start next Wednesday. Does anyone have anything new they would like to report?"

All was quiet. Bert then said, "Well, this might be one of the shortest meetings in our history! All I can tell you is to keep going on your searches if you haven't yet finished your area. Also, I can tell you that I did hear from CIA Director Rudy Lester saying that for sure the rocket is an Aerobee 170A, but that's nothing new to us since we already had the size and weight. Also, we know the guy that stole the rocket was from Wallops Island, Virginia. His name is Ralph Keelen, but he has the nickname Geek. He's mid thirties, average height and weight, and when last seen he had a pony tail, full beard, and wore thick glasses. But he's likely changed that appearance. Other than that, nothing new on my end. Let's call our meeting adjourned and you guys get back out there. I certainly appreciate all your efforts."

The deputies filed out, leaving the two agents and Sheriff Sterling. Sammy King said, "Guys, other than Bennie Sekao, that BSC operation up on Black Mountain has two employees. The one guy, Max, had a pretty strong accent. The other guy, Ralph, fits the description that we have for Ralph Keelen minus the pony tail, beard, and glasses. He certainly could have shaved his head and face and gotten contact lens. I know it's a stretch, but we also know someone brought in the warhead, and that could have been this Max guy. I'm just speculating here, but Director Lester did suggest we might want to pay another visit to BSC and look around a bit more. What do you think?"

Bert thought for a minute, then said, "Not a bad idea. I'm with Sammy thinking that something just doesn't seem right there. Also, when Sammy visited there before he didn't have a Geiger Counter. Now that we've got those, maybe we should indeed pay them another visit."

Agent Cody Short said, "I like it. And why don't the three of us go up there right now. It's only 4 o'clock, we could be there in about 30 minutes. And maybe we should start playing a little more hard ball. Two G-men and the sheriff might make them a tad nervous if they're bad guys hiding a rocket."

The three then all nodded in agreement, and Bert said, "Let's do it. I'll drive, you two can just ride with me."

They walked to Bert's cruiser, got in, and headed for Black Mountain.

• • •

30 Minutes Later
BSC site
Black Mountain, Kentucky

Bennie Sekao, sitting at his desk, said, "Guys, I know it's a tad early, but I got a couple of errands I need to run before going home. If you don't object I think I'm going to head toward Harlan."

Ralph Neleek said, "No problem, Bennie, you go right ahead, and you have a great weekend."

Max looked over at the monitors and said, "You might have to wait a minute, Bennie, there's a car approaching..... and it looks like Sheriff Sterling."

All three watched the monitors as Bert, then Cody, and then Sammy got out of the cruiser. Ralph said, "That don't look good....three of em."

Bennie replied, "Oh, they're probably just on a social call."

Max looked at Ralph. The two got very worried looks on their faces. Bennie ran to the door to let them in.

"Hey guys," Bennie said, "come right in, come right in. You paying us a social visit?"

The three lawmen looked dead serious. Bert replied, "Sorry Bennie, afraid not. When Agent King was here before we didn't have some equipment that we've since acquired. We'd like to look around again. We're still looking for that big drug shipment, and this remote site would be a great place for the bad guys to hide it. You all wouldn't even know it. I hope you don't object to us just having another look around?"

Max looked at Ralph, and the two shrugged their shoulders. Bennie said, "I don't think that would be a problem at all, would it fellows?"

Ralph answered, "No, no problem. Where would you like to start?"

Sammy King said, "We'll get our drug sniffing instruments out of the car and then come back in here, if that's okay?"

Bennie said, "Guys, if you don't mind I have some errands to run. I think I'll walk out with you and then take off for Harlan. Unless you need me?"

All nodded in agreement. The law men and Bennie went out the door. Ralph and Max were left in the office alone. Ralph looked at Max and said, "I'm beginning to get a headache! This looks bad!"

Max replied, "Don't worry Ralph. We're covered. The only way they could find anything would be for one of them to shimmy 30 foot up that hollow column and look down in it. And that's not going to happen!"

Ralph said, "Yeah, I know. But I still worry that they might see something. We gotta be really careful what we say."

The lawmen then came back through the door, each carrying their Geiger Counter, aka drug sniffer. Bert said, "Guys, we'll just start here in the office, then go out to the columns, and then check the storage building.....if that's okay."

Ralph spoke, "That's fine. Except when we get to the storage building I'll have to see Top Secret clearances from everyone."

"That I do not have," the sheriff said. "But Cody and Sammy do and they can check everything inside there."

"Fine," replied Ralph. "You guys just go right ahead and look all you wish. When you're finished here we can go outside.

The three lawmen walked throughout the office building with their Geiger Counters. After about 10 minutes all assembled back at the desks. Bert said, "All's fine here. Let's head outside."

All five walked outside to the column construction site. "Those sure are impressive," Bert said. "You just don't see concrete columns 30 feet high very often. And four of them."

The law men all walked around each column holding their Geiger Counters. They then walked over all the concrete pad upon which the columns were build.

"Nothing here", Bert finally said. "You guys go over and check out the storage building, I'll snoop around here a little longer."

The four men walked to the storage building. Ralph then looked at Agent Short. Cody dug out his credential wallet and flipped it open. Ralph nodded when he saw the Top Secret clearance. Ralph entered the code for the overhead door and it opened. The two agents carried their instruments all around inside the building. First they checked out the four boxes of electronic equipment, then they walked to the back wall where the pipes were resting one above the other on the brackets attached to the back wall.

Sammy said, "When I was here before these pipes were on the floor. I see you've now put brackets on the wall for em."

Ralph replied, "Yeah, that's right. Trying to conserve floor space."

Sammy nodded. At the same time Cody's instrument starting making a clicking noise as he held it toward one end of the uppermost pipe. The two agents then stuck their heads at either end of that pipe and looked into it. Each saw the other's face at the other end. Sammy laughed and said, "No drugs in there. Must just be a false reading."

After a few more minutes of passing the counters over the floor and walls Sammy said, "Okay guys, we're all drug free here. Unless the sheriff's turned up something we'll get out of here and let you close up shop."

Max and Ralph nodded. They all walked out the overhead door, with Max pushing the button to close it on his way.

They then walked back to the office building. Bert was standing outside the entrance door. He had already stowed his Geiger Counter. He said, "Everything good in the storage building?"

Cody and Sammy nodded yes. The lawmen then shook hands with Max and Ralph, and thanked them. Max and Ralph then turned and started walking back to the office building.

Suddenly Bert shouted, "Hey, Geek!"

Ralph jerked his head around with a frightened look at Bert.

Bert pointed to the concrete columns and said, "Big concrete!"

Ralph and Max smiled, then entered the office building.

Once inside Ralph asked Max, "Did what the sheriff shouted the first time sound like 'big concrete' to you?"

Max said, "I wasn't paying attention. I don't know?"

"It sounded like 'Hey Geek' to me," Ralph said.

"So what?" asked Max.

"My nickname at Wallops Island was 'Geek'," replied Ralph.

"Maybe you're hearing things," Max said as the two turned out the lights and headed back out the door.

Ralph said, "Maybe.........maybe not."

The two walked toward their cars. They then stopped as Max said, "I'll tell you one thing. Those instruments they were using were not drug sniffers. They were Geiger Counters. I've used them enough to know one when I see and hear it. That reading they got from the back wall in the storage building was residual radiation from our warhead. I think they now know for sure that there was something radioactive in that building. Fortunately for us, the warhead is now 30 feet above the ground and surrounded by about an inch of concrete all around. That's why they didn't get any readings when they checked the bottom of the columns."

Ralph replied, "Well, I guess we can safely assume they are onto us. Do you think there's any chance a plane, chopper, or even a satellite could pick up the hollow column and the warhead in it?"

"No way," Max said. "Even satellites don't have that kind of resolution. And a plane is just traveling too fast to be able to see it. A chopper could, but with all the trees around our site they couldn't get very close. I think we're safe there."

Ralph said, "Five days to go. We've just got to hold it together until then. The good thing for us is that the law can't do anything without proof, and we've got that rocket well hidden. We're just going to have to be super careful for the next five days."

They each got in their cars to drive off Black Mountain.

. . .

At the same time
Black Mountain, Kentucky

As Bert drove his cruiser down Black Mountain he said, "Did you see Ralph jerk his head around when I called for Geek? I think we've found Ralph Keelen, aka Geek Keelen, aka Ralph Neleek."

Sammy and Cody nodded. Sammy said, "I think you're right. And I think the warhead was stored at one time on that back wall in the storage building. It left some residual radiation. That's what my counter was picking up. They've moved it somewhere."

"But where the heck is it? Nothing else showed anything," Bert said.

Cody said, "Yeah, it's frustrating. We think we got the bad guys, but we can't find their 3000 pound, 40 foot long rocket! But we have definitely made good progress. At least we now are almost sure that we know those are the two that brought the rocket and the warhead into Harlan County. We've just got to locate them. Do you suppose they might be set up somewhere other than at the BSC site?"

The sheriff replied, "It's possible. But if so they sure went to a lot of trouble building those huge concrete columns. Why would they do that?"

Sammy said, "Yeah, doesn't make sense. Intuition just tells me that they're at the BSC site somewhere."

Bert replied, "I know the construction company that erected those columns. They are a company called Tackett Construction and are out of Knoxville. They've done several jobs in Harlan, and I know were involved in the construction of the concrete tunnels that diverted a river through a mountain as part of our flood control program. I think I'll give them a call tomorrow to see if I can find out anything unusual about the construction of those columns. I think somehow they have to be the key."

Agent Cody said, "Sounds like a good idea to me. In the meantime I'll report what happened today at BSC to Director Lester. He said he'd be checking them out. Maybe he's come up with something too."

"Guys, with time running so short why don't we plan to get together tomorrow at about 4 pm in my office. We need to give everything some thought and plan out our next moves. I think we're getting close!"

Both Agents said, "Will do."

Bert reached the bottom of Black Mountain and continued toward Harlan.

Chapter 21

Present Time

November 23

Harlan, Kentucky

Sheriff J. Bert Sterling sat at his desk at 9 am on Saturday morning. He had just disconnected his cell phone from a conversation with the secretary at Tackett Construction Company in Knoxville. He had inquired from the secretary, who luckily worked on Saturday mornings, the name of the person in charge of the work at the BSC site on Black Mountain. He was told that a Mr. Roger Gates was in charge of the project, but that Mr. Gates was not in the office. He had taken his son camping in the Smokies for the weekend but should be back at work on Monday. Bert asked for his cell phone number and the secretary said that Mr. Gates had told her he would be taking his cell phone with him for use in an emergency, but would have it turned off because he didn't want to be disturbed while spending time with his son. The sheriff then inquired if anyone else there in the office or that he could phone would be knowledgeable about the project. She replied that Mr. Gates was the only one with all the plans and information about the construction. The other Tackett people there just followed Mr. Gates' directions. After thanking the nice secretary, Bert called the cell phone of Roger Gates and it immediately went to his recording. Bert left a message for him to please call him the first chance he got.

As Bert sat and thought about their situation Rosie knocked on his door, cracked it open and said, "Bert, Trigger Green is here to see you."

Bert stood and said, "Great. Please send him in."

Trigger walked in, shook hands with the sheriff, and the two took seats. Bert asked, "Trigger, it's a beautiful fall day out there today. What brings you in to see me?"

Trigger replied, "Bert, I've been giving a lot of thought to our conversation about that rocket. It really scares me. If I thought I had anything whatsoever to do with it I'd never forgive myself. And I still am not sure at all about it....I've thought and thought about things that have happened over the past year or so, and still nothing about a rocket registers. But I did think of one situation that just could fit....but I'm certainly not sure....it's just intuition more than anything else."

"I'd sure like to hear it," Bert said. "Sometimes our intuition is right on target."

Trigger continued, "Well, close to a year ago I got a phone call from someone I'll keep unnamed asking me to assist with a project. He told me a company wanted to build an antenna on top of Black Mountain and asked if I would look for property up there and help get a lease and then assist with getting prefab buildings arranged. He offered me a substantial fee to do this, so I certainly didn't see anything wrong with doing it. Heck, it didn't even sound illegal. So that was how the Beck Signal Corporation, or BSC, site got underway. The caller also asked for help in locating one employee for them, and I was told that there would be two additional BSC employees. I recommended Bennie Sekao, and that's how he got his job. I was then told that one of the BSC employees, a fellow named Ralph Neleek, would be coming to the site and would stop by here on his way to pick up the keys to the buildings. When he arrived, about 6 months ago, he'd been driving overnight and also wanted to nap a while before going on his way. He was driving a rental van. It certainly couldn't have contained a

40 foot rocket, but I got to thinking about maybe the thing could be disassembled into smaller lengths. I'm sure the truck he had could have hauled pieces 10 or 15 feet long. I certainly didn't see in the truck, and I really have no reason to believe such a thought, but it was just something that occurred to me. The more I thought about it the more curious I got. So very early this morning, around 6 am, I drove up to Black Mountain to have a look around. I got there well before the two employees would show up, and being Saturday I didn't even know if they would. I did know Bennie didn't usually work on Saturdays. So I got there and spent about an hour walking all around the property. I didn't find anything that remotely looked like a rocket. Other than the office and storage buildings, the only things there are those four monster concrete columns. Oh, there were two other things. My contact had requested that I get two old cars and deliver them up there. And they were parked there. I don't have any idea why he requested them, but he wanted them to be old and reliable. So I guess it was a wasted trip. But on the way back I just decided I'd drop by and share my thoughts with you, for what they're worth....possibly nothing."

"Trigger, I think your instinct is working! We are now almost certain that those two guys working there, Neleek and Baker, are involved with the rocket. We have information from the CIA that Neleek was carrying the rocket segments in that rental van, and that Baker likely was the person that brought the warhead. What you've just told me fits into the puzzle perfectly. But the problem we still have is that we can't locate the rocket. We've searched the buildings thoroughly, finding nothing. And as you say, the only other things there are those concrete columns. We're thinking about another look all around the site maybe tomorrow. Sunday should be dead up there. We thought that just maybe they had the rocket set up somewhere else on their property but away from the main site. What are your thoughts about that?"

Trigger thought for a moment and replied, "I guess it's possible. But how would you lug a 3000 pound, 40 foot rocket through all those trees and then set it up? Anything's possible, but it doesn't seem likely to me."

"Yeah, that's about what I thought as well," the sheriff replied. "But frankly, we don't know what else to do at this point. We don't have anything concrete to arrest Neleek and Baker for, and if we did they'd likely clam up. And for all we know that rocket could be all set and will fire at the appointed time with or without those two. So, that's about where we are. I do have a phone call into the guy in charge of constructing those concrete columns. He works for Tackett Construction in Knoxville. But it'll likely be Monday before I hear from him. We'll continue to work all leads, but our time is running out."

Trigger shook his head, stood, and said, "I'll continue to give it thought. If I come up with anything I'll call you. Thanks for listening to me. At least my conscience feels better!!"

Bert replied, "Trigger, you are a good citizen. I really appreciate what you told me. It does help to fit things together, and do keep thinking and keep your eyes and ears open for anything new."

The two shook hands and Trigger left for Maggard's Grocery.

About an hour later

Bert walked into the front office. Rosie was off for the weekend. Deputy Kyle Potter was sitting at his desk. Preacher Puss had jumped down and was sitting in Kyle's lap. She was being given loving strokes by the deputy. She purred her approval as she swished her long tail.

"Hey Kyle, it's about lunch time. Want to go over to Creech's and grab something to eat?"

Kyle gently lifted Preacher Puss back up to her bed on the wall shelf and said, "Best suggestion I've heard today. Maybe ole Fred can cheer us up."

The two walked across Central Street to Creech Cafe.

After stroking and paying proper attention to Polly, Bert and Kyle spotted the Mayor sitting at a table in the back with Pastor Raymond Bell. They walked back to their table. Fred looked up, saw them, and said, "Boys, please join us."

After passing a few pleasantries, Bert said, "Raymond, it is truly good to see you. I was thinking about coming over to the church for a visit, but the Lord has put us together here at Creech Cafe."

Raymond Bell, pastor of the Harlan Baptist Church, said, "Well, the Lord works in mysterious ways. Here we are. Was what you wanted to say to me private, or would it be okay for Fred and Kyle to hear?"

"It's certainly not private," Bert replied. "But it is a little unusual. I can't really tell you precisely what it is, but we have a very serious problem and are having a most difficult time finding a solution. It involves lots of people, some possibly being killed and many others with injuries. I thought perhaps you could say some appropriate words in church tomorrow without scaring the congregation, and ask for the Lord's help."

Pastor Bell replied, "It is indeed a bit unusual, Bert, but I'll be happy to give it thought and prayer, and will then ask everyone tomorrow to plead for His help.

Bert replied, "Thanks Raymond. You've heard the ole adage 'We need all the help we can get'. Well, with our current problem it certainly applies."

Pastor Bell smiled, stood, and said, "In order to receive, one must first ask. And ask we shall. I hate to run but I've got to work on my sermon, and now to also give thought to exactly how to present the problem to the congregation. Keep me in your prayers."

All nodded in agreement as Raymond walked toward the door.

Fred looked at Bert and Kyle and said, "From that I take it that our problem has not yet been solved."

Kyle and Bert shook their heads. Bert said, "It has not. And the holidays start next Wednesday. It's really strange, we're almost certain we know that BSC operation is involved. We just can't locate the rocket, and without it we have little leverage to apply to Neleek and Baker. They're in it, we just don't know the details. We do plan to go up to the site tomorrow and snoop around some more, but I'm not very hopeful."

Bert then told Fred about the call he had in to the Tackett Construction guy. Just then Bert's cell phone rang. He answered, "Sheriff Sterling."

Fred and Kyle watched and listened as Bert talked. When the call was over the sheriff said, "That call was from CIA Director Rudy Lester. He said after looking into BSC they have concluded it's a phony. They have a Houston address, but when it was checked out it turned out to be a pizza shop. Good to know, but we suspected that anyway. Bottom line is, we've got to find that rocket."

After eating lunch, feeding crumbs to Polly, and small-talking for another 10 minutes Kyle said, "Fred, we need cheered. Got anything?"

Fred thought a moment, then said, "I heard one from old Doc Spenzer this morning. Three elderly men were in a nursing home. One said '70 is the worst age. You always feel like you have to pee, and most of the time you stand at the toilet and nothing comes out'. The 80 year old said, 'That's nothing. When you get to 80 you take laxatives and eat bran and then sit on the toilet all day and nothing comes out'. The 90 year old replied, 'Just wait until you're 90. I pee a bucket full every morning at 6 am, and then have a super bowel movement every morning at 6:30am. And then at 10 am I wake up.'"

Kyle and Bert laughed, slapped Fred on the back, and Kyle said, "Now we're leaving with smiles on our faces. Thanks Mr. Mayor

• • •

Same day, 4 pm
Sheriff's office
Harlan, Kentucky

Agents Short and King, Deputy Kyle Potter, and Sheriff Sterling were gathered in the sheriff's office to plan their next move.

Bert first explained the visit from Trigger Green, the phone call from Director Lester, and the phone call to Tackett Construction. He also said that Pastor Bell and his congregation would be asking for help from above, without knowing specifically what the problem was. He then said, "So, we got only three days before the Thanksgiving holidays start. I still think we should go up to the BSC site tomorrow and snoop all around, particularly checking the property that surrounds the cleared site. Who knows, maybe they have sneaked that dadburn rocket somewhere else. But if we don't have luck tomorrow, lets talk about what we do on our last two days....Monday and Tuesday."

The G-men nodded agreement. Sammy King then said, "Yeah, I definitely think we need to have a good game plan at the end. We've just got to come up with some way to find where the rocket is hidden."

"Here's my suggestion," Bert said. "If we fail to find anything tomorrow, let's all four go back up to BSC on

Monday morning, early. Let's walk into the office and lay our cards on the table. Let's tell the three of them what we know and what we think. I'm pretty sure they won't be able to convince us that they're innocent, but maybe the shock of hearing what we know will be enough to cause them to let something slip that will lead to the rocket. What do you think?"

"I like it," Kyle said. "Enough pussyfooting around. Let's see what they have to say."

The G-men nodded in agreement. Cody Short said, "I don't see that it could hurt. Let's plan on it."

"If Monday fails, we only got the one day left," Bert said. "You guys think real hard on what we should do if we arrive on Tuesday without anything. So unless you got something else, I'll meet you at the BSC site tomorrow morning at about 8 am.....that okay?"

Everyone nodded agreement, stood, and headed out of the sheriff's office. Kyle Potter went back to his desk. The two G-men looked at Preacher Puss as they approached the door. Both saluted her and went to their car.

Chapter 22

Present Time, November 24

BSC site

Black Mountain, Kentucky

The two cars arrived at the BSC site, one driven by Sheriff Sterling, the other by Agent Sammy King. They pulled up in front of the office building, got out, and stood together.

Bert said, "It sure is quiet up here on this Sunday morning. So peaceful....only the sound of birds chirping and wind in the trees. Hard to believe there might be a rocket with a nuclear warhead around somewhere!"

"Not a pleasant thought," Agent Short said. "But it's our job to find out. What's the game plan?"

"Well, we've all got our Geiger counters. Let's just fan out into four different quadrants and sniff around with our counters and keep our eyes open for anything out of the ordinary. We need to go well beyond just the cleared site here....Let's go into the woods for maybe a quarter mile each to see if we see any signs of anything in there. Let's plan to meet back here in about an hour."

The four moved out, each in a different direction.

One hour later

The four again stood together in front of the office building. Bert said, "I take it from the looks on your faces that nothing was discovered?"

All nodded agreement. Agent Sammy King said, "I know that damn rocket is 40 feet long, and I know that those concrete columns are only 30 feet high, but they're still suspicious to me. They just have to have something to do with the rocket. Maybe they removed one stage from it....shortening it to 30 feet or less. You think that possible?"

Bert shrugged his shoulders and said, "Anything's possible. But all we can see here are four huge 30 foot high concrete columns. What do you suggest?"

Sammy replied, "We can't see the tops of them. I'd sure like to take a look down from above."

Deputy Kyle Potter said, "How can we do that? The truck boom that was here during their construction is gone. Unless one of you guys know how to shimmy up a 30 foot concrete column I don't know how we could do it. A chopper is out of the question....those trees all around just make bringing one in too chancy."

The sheriff thought a moment and then said, "You know, I've seen power and telephone people using extension ladders that were mighty long. They're really heavy, and take at least two people to move them, but they are available. Maybe I could check with Kentucky Utilities tomorrow and see if they have one we could borrow. I think Sammy's right. The columns have to be the key. And hopefully I'll hear from Tackett Construction tomorrow as well."

Agent Short said, "Any of you think of anything else we could accomplish up here today?"

Bert said, "No, I think we should head back home. But I'll tell you one thing, I'll not be resting when I get there. I'll be thinking about this whole situation and trying to come up with something new. And I would encourage each of you to do the same."

All nodded, got in their cars, and started the drive back down Black Mountain and home.

• • •

Same time
Pyongyang, North Korea

Chairman Kim sat at his desk having a late snack of two big macs and a large order of fries. General Ri sat erect on the sofa to Kim's right. The chairman, between bites, said, "General, time is growing really, really close. Just 3 days to go before the world recognizes me and North Korea as THE world leader. Everything you hear from Kentucky okay?"

General Ri replied, "Absolutely, Chairman Kim. Our plan of putting the rocket in the hollow concrete column has worked to perfection. It has not been discovered, and all the plans to fire it on Wednesday are a 'go'. It should launch at exactly 7 pm Kentucky time, which will be 8 am on Thanksgiving morning here in Pyongyang. What a wonderful Thanksgiving gift it will be to you."

Kim continued to chew his food. He looked at the general and said, "Ri, are you absolutely sure no one suspects anything?"

"Absolutely, Chairman Kim."

Kim continued to eat and looked at Ri and said, "You better be. If this comes off as planned you'll be greatly rewarded. Many more metals and more money. But if it doesn't, you'll either be hung, shot, or sent to prison for hard labor for the rest of your life." Kim smiled at Ri as he finished a french fry.

The general said, "I understand, Chairman Kim."

• • •

Same time
The White House
Washington, D.C.

President DeVore sat behind his desk in the oval office. CIA Director Rudy Lester sat in a chair in front of the desk.

The president shook his head and said, "Down to three days, Rudy. I do understand we're making some apparent progress, but we still have not located the rocket. Do you and/or the other cabinet heads have any alternate game plan if on Wednesday we haven't found it.?"

"Some," Director Lester replied. "We have moved into position some anti-ballistic missiles. But whether or not they could take out the Aerobee is a bit of a question. Once the Aerobee is fired, it will cover the 125 mile journey to its apogee in about 2 minutes at an average speed of about 4,000 mph. Our ABM's are good, but they could certainly miss their target. We also will have aircraft ready to go on Wednesday. They will carry bombs and rockets, and, if ordered to do so, could take out any site where the rocket was thought to be."

President DeVore said, "I like the ABM's. I don't care for the bombs and/or rockets. Too much chance to hit civilians and private property and to miss the rocket. Anything else?"

"I think that's about it, Mr. President. The best scenario is for our guys to locate the rocket and disarm or disable it. And we do still have 3 days to do that. They are working hard."

"Rudy, I want you to call me the second you find out anything new on this thing. I don't think I'm going to be sleeping real well till that rocket is neutralized."

Chapter 23

Present Time,

November 25

Harlan, Kentucky

"Morning Rosie," both Bert and Kyle said as they walked through the entrance door to the sheriff's department. They had just had their morning coffee at Creech Cafe.

"Hi Guys," Rosie said. "Hope the weekend wasn't too bad."

"It could have been a lot better if we'd come up with that rocket," Kyle said. The two men then walked into Bert's office and took a seat.

After chatting for a few minutes Bert's cell phone rang. He pressed the button to accept the call, then said, "Sheriff Sterling."

The voice at the other end said, "Good morning Sheriff, this is Roger Gates with Tackett Construction in Knoxville. I just turned my cell phone back on and saw where you had called. I'm sorry to be so late returning your call. What can I do for you?"

Bert said, "Mr. Gates, thanks so much for returning my call. I hope you had a great weekend with your son in those beautiful Smoky Mountains."

"Well, thank you. We had a super time. Unfortunately I don't get that much time to spend with him, and it turned out to be one of those really magical times together. I appreciate your asking."

Bert said, "So good to hear. The reason I was calling has to do with the four 30 foot concrete columns you guys just finished constructing at the BSC site on Black Mountain. Your secretary said you were the person that was most familiar with them, and I had a few questions."

"Certainly," Mr. Gates replied.

"Lets start with the basics," said the sheriff. "My understanding is that each of the four were constructed to support a platform that will be constructed atop them, and that the platform will in turn be the base for a huge antenna that will be built. Is that your understanding?"

"It is," said Mr. Gates.

Bert continued, "My understanding is that each column is about 4 feet in diameter. Do you know anything abnormal about any of these columns? Anything out of the ordinary?"

There was a pause on the other end, and then Mr. Gates said, "Well, the only thing different about any of them is that the North West column is hollow. The other three are solid concrete."

Bert about fell out of his chair. He recovered and asked, "Now why would that be?"

Mr. Gates said, "Mr. Neleek said that they needed the space to pass cables and wiring down from the antenna. I really didn't question him. I just built them to his specs."

"What size was the hollow space," Bert asked.

"As you said, the outside diameter was 4 feet. The walls were 11 inches thick, so that left a hollow column about 26 inches in diameter," Gates replied.

"So the hole in the center of the North West column is a little over 2 feet in diameter. That sure could handle a lot of cable and wiring!" Bert said.

Gates replied, "Yeah, I thought it a little strange myself. But they kept talking about how secret the whole project was so I didn't ask many questions. I figured surely they knew what they were doing."

"Mr. Gates, I can't thank you enough for your help. This information is very helpful. Is there anything else you think of that didn't seem right?"

"As a matter of fact, now that I think about it, there was," he said. "Under that same North West column they had us dig a 11 foot deep hole and pour a one foot thick concrete pad at the bottom. I didn't even ask what it was for....I figured it was secret."

Bert then about dropped the phone! He said, "Boy, you are providing us answers to questions that we just couldn't figure out. You've been a true blessing for us. Thanks so much for sharing with us. Next time you're in Harlan drop by the office and I'll take you out for a steak dinner!"

Mr. Gates replied, "Well, I'm glad the information will help you. Always happy to assist the law. You have a good day, sheriff."

"You know, I think I will!" Bert replied as he disconnected the call.

Kyle looked at Bert. Although the deputy had only heard Bert's side of the conversation it was enough for him to piece together what was said. The two men had big smiles on their faces as they stood and patted each other on the back. Bert said, "Now I think we know where that rocket is. We now need to find some way to look inside the North West column. Once we confirm it's there we can get a warrant to shut that site down and destroy the rocket."

Kyle said, "As you were talking to Mr. Gates I got an idea. I know we're going to try and get a long extension ladder from Kentucky Utilities, but another way I think would work would be to take my drone plane up there. It's got a pretty good camera on it, and I bet I could hover it directly over that column and we could see down in it. It might be a lot easier than getting the ladder and lugging it up there.....what'd you think?"

"Great idea, Kyle. I've watched you fly that thing, and you got it down pretty good. Can you watch what the camera sees on a screen on the ground?"

"Sure can, Bert. My controller has a small screen that shows what the camera sees. That'll not be a problem."

Bert replied, "Hey, I'm beginning to feel good about this whole thing. Why don't you go home and pick up the drone. I'll contact the G-men and tell them the developments. And I'll ask Cody to call Director Lester and update him. And then let's all plan to meet at the BSC site at 2 pm. Will that work with you?"

Kyle said, "That should work. I know I need to charge the batteries in my drone before we use it. I'll run home and plug it in. They should charge up pretty quickly. I feel certain I can do that and get up Black Mountain by 2 pm."

"Super. See you at 2."

. . .

Earlier that day
Benham, Kentucky

Ralph and Max had just finished their breakfast at the Benham Hotel, and were walking to Ralph's car to drive up to the site. Max was riding with Ralph today. When in their car Ralph said, "I gotta tell you Max, I'm really getting nervous. Day after tomorrow at 7 pm we light up that rocket, but I just know the sheriff and those G-men are getting close to discovering us. You got the same feeling?"

Max nodded and said, "I do. But surely we can hold them off two more days. We've just got to do it. Ralph, tell me again exactly how we go about firing the rocket."

Ralph said, "It's pretty straight forward. You've seen it's control console, it's only about the size of a hand-held tablet computer. It's already programmed to fire at 7 pm on Wednesday unless aborted. Once it's fired the payload will reach it's highest point, or apogee, in about 2 minutes. Then the big bang, and we get off this mountain and get on with our lives."

"Question," Max said. "What if the rocket malfunctions and doesn't fire for some reason. Wouldn't the warhead then detect the lack of motion and think the rocket had reached its peak and detonate the bomb?"

"Well, it would," Ralph said. "But if that happened I would have 5 seconds to press the red button on the console that would deactivate the warhead. I forgot to tell you before that once the apogee is reached there is a 5 second delay until detonation. So if the rocket just didn't fire, I'd still have 5 seconds to push that red button and prevent our being blown up."

"That's comforting to know," Max said. "Is there some way you know the 5 second count down has begun?"

"Oh yeah. There is a yellow bulb on the console that starts to blink when the bomb is 5 seconds from explosion. After that nothing will stop the detonation."

Max thought a moment and then said, "So why do we have to be at the site when all this takes place? Couldn't we already be on our way out of here?"

"No, the console has to be within 100 yards of the rocket to work. But the red button signal to abort utilizes satellite technology and works at any distance. So should we need to stop the bomb anytime after the rocket's launch we could, just so long as it was before the 5 seconds after reaching apogee. And the reason for the console to be within 100 yards to work is so that if rocket failure occurred we would know it and be able to stop the bomb explosion. If we were miles away there would be no way to know the rocket didn't fire."

"Sure sounds complicated," Max replied. "But thanks for explaining it to me. We just need to be there at the site at 7 pm on Wednesday. By 7:02 we'll be headed down the mountain!"

. . .

Noon, that same day
The Oval Office
Washington, D. C.

President DeVore replaced the phone, stood, started dancing around the Oval Office shouting "Thank you Lord, Thank you Lord."

A secret service agent posted outside the Oval Office door heard the commotion and came rushing in. He said, "You okay Mr. President?"

"Boy, am I ever," the president replied. The agent left the room. President DeVore thought: That phone call from Director Lester was the best news I've been given in a long time. Surely that rocket is stuck down in that hollow concrete column. All that now has to be done to get this whole thing over is for them to positively identify it, shut the site down, and deactivate the rocket. Thank you Jesus!"

. . .

Same day, 2 pm
BSC site
Black Mountain, Kentucky

Bennie, Ralph, and Max were sitting at their desks chatting. Max saw three cars approaching as he glanced at the monitors. He said, "Guys, we got company again. It looks like the law, and three cars this time." They watched as Bert, Agents Short and King, and Deputy Kyle Potter got out of their cars. Kyle was carrying a large box of some kind.

Bennie rushed to the door, opened it, and greeted the men, "Hey guys, come right on in. Good to see you all. Kyle, what you got in that big box?"

Kyle replied, "We're going to talk about that, Bennie."

Ralph and Max nodded to the group. Ralph said, "You guys are frequent visitors up here recently. What's up now?"

Sheriff Sterling said, "We had another idea on looking for where those drugs might be hidden. Deputy Potter here has a drone plane, and we'd like to fly it over the property here to see if we can detect any spots that look like they've been recently disturbed....maybe the drugs are buried. Any objection?"

Max looked at Ralph with a scared expression. Ralph thought for a minute and then said, "I guess that would be okay. How long will it take?"

"Don't know, maybe an hour or two," Kyle replied.

"Okay, let us know if you need help," Ralph said.

Bennie joined the other four and walked outside the office building. Max and Ralph remained seated at their desks. After the door was closed Max said, "Why did you agree to let them fly that drone. They'll take it over the column with the rocket and see it."

Ralph grinned and said, "You'd think that. But as it turns out, I'm very familiar with that drone. I noticed the brand and model from the box. Our glider club back at Wallops Island used to fly them frequently, and we had one just like the one the deputy has. The camera on it is pretty good, but not good enough to pick up the warhead in the column. That warhead is painted black, and I'm sure the camera doesn't have the resolution to pick it up. The tip of the warhead is about a foot down from the top of the column anyway. So if they look directly down from the top of the column they'll only see a black hole.....no rocket. So that's why I agreed for them to go ahead and fly the thing. Don't worry."

Max then smiled and said, "I sure hope you're right. But I am still worried!"

Outside, Kyle was getting the drone all set up. Bennie was watching with great interest. He said, "Kyle, I never saw one of those things before. This should be real interesting!"

Kyle answered, "Yeah, Bennie, I think you'll enjoy watching. Drones are neat."

Once the drone was all set up Kyle placed it on the ground. He then picked up its flight controller, pushed a few buttons, and the drone propellers started to turn. The machine then slowly started to rise from the ground, swaying slightly from side to side.

Max and Ralph were watching closely by viewing the security monitors inside the office.

The drone continued to move upward. The group was standing about midway between the office and storage buildings. Kyle then started to maneuver the aircraft over toward the four concrete columns in back of the office building. The drone was several feet above the tops of the columns. It then passed over the South East column on a diagonal headed for the North West. All the guys were clustered around Kyle, watching the small screen on the controller. When Kyle had positioned the drone directly over the North West column he held it motionless. Everyone looked at the image from its camera on the controller screen. What they saw was the rim of the column, but inside that column they only could see a black hole.

Bert said, "Can you get it a little closer, Kyle?"

Kyle said, "I'll try, but it's about as close as I can hold it." He lowered the drone slightly, but the camera still only showed the round concrete rim surrounding a jet black hole. Nothing could be seen in the column.

Inside the office building Ralph said, "They've talked to the Tackett Construction people. They went straight to that North West column. They knew it was hollow, but they're not seeing anything."

The sheriff then said, "Kyle, can you change the camera settings to get any more definition in the hollow part?"

"Sorry, Bert, but I don't have the ability to do any adjustments to the camera. Maybe some of the more expensive and elaborate models have that capability, but on this one what you see is what you get."

The G-men shook their heads. Cody then said, "It was a good try. And we know it's in there, but the drone just can't identify it for us."

Bert said, "You're right, Cody, I think we're still going to have to get that ladder."

Bennie said, "You guys think the drugs are stuffed down in that column?"

Bert replied, "Bennie, we can't really tell you more about our investigation, I hope you understand."

"Sure, Bert, I do understand. It's official business."

The G-men, Kyle, and Bert all smiled. "Thanks for understanding, Bennie," answered Bert.

Kyle retrieved his drone and boxed it up. Everyone walked back to the office building and entered. Max looked up and said, "Find any drugs with that drone?"

Bert said, "No, but we suspect that hollow column. We plan to get a long extension ladder and come back and check it out.....that okay?"

Ralph grinned and said, "No problem, sheriff. We want to cooperate anyway we can."

"See you a little later then," Bert said as the law guys departed.

Once outside the office building Bert told the group, "Guys, I'm going to get in contact with Kentucky Utilities and see if we can't get them to bring up one of those big ladders. My guess is it'll be too late today....and it'll be getting dark before long anyway. So, likely it'll be tomorrow before we can get it. But I feel absolutely certain when someone gets to the top of that North West column and shines a flashlight down inside they'll see the head of a rocket. We've still got time.....and we're going to make it work."

All departed down Black Mountain.

Chapter 24

Present Time

November 25

Harlan, Kentucky

The Sheriff sat at his desk. It was late. Rosie had left a couple of hours ago. He thought:

We are now down to just one more full day before the first Thanksgiving holiday on Wednesday. Kentucky Utilities was very cooperative and said they would have a truck with a large ladder at the BSC site tomorrow, but that it couldn't get there until after lunch....likely around 2. That's cutting it close, but it should work. And besides, I don't think of any other options.

. . .

Same time
the Oval Office
Washington, D. C.

President DeVore sat at his desk with his elbows on the desk and his head resting in his hands. He had just received a call from Director Lester telling him of the day's events on Black Mountain. He thought: They still haven't found the dadburn rocket! And I know it's in that one hollow column, and I know they'll certainly identify it tomorrow.....but we're almost on our deadline, and so many lives are at risk here. I think it's time for me to talk with the man upstairs.

. . .

Present time
November 26
Black Mountain, Kentucky

All four law officials were in the Sheriff's cruiser. They just pulled up in front of the BSC office building. It was just a few minutes before 2 pm. The Kentucky Utilities truck had not yet arrived. The four got out, walked to the door and knocked.

Bennie Sekao greeted them, "Ralph and Max have been wondering when you would return….and here you are!"

Bert replied, "Hi Bennie, please take a seat at your desk. This is certainly not a social call." He looked at Ralph and Max seated at their desks, and nodded.

Ralph spoke, "Sheriff, we're really getting a little tired of this little game. You and your men have been here several times and have found nothing. Surely you're not back again today to look around again."

"Yes, and no," Bert said. "We are here to look around, but only in one place. We'll just quit playing games and tell you that we think you have an Aerobee rocket hidden out there in the North West column. We think your real name is Ralph Keelen, and that your buddy Max here brought a nuclear warhead into our country. All we've got to do is identify that rocket and you two will be under arrest. So that's the purpose of our trip today. Any thoughts?"

Ralph chuckled and said, "My name is Ralph Neleek, and Max here is simply a BSC employee and knows nothing about any nuclear warhead, right Max?"

Max simply nodded in agreement.

"Have it your own way, Mr. Keelen," the sheriff replied, "but the game's over. We have a Kentucky Utilities truck on the way here carrying a long extension ladder. We're going to lean it against that North West column, climb it, and look down with a flashlight and identify the rocket. Your goose will then be cooked."

"My, my....aren't we testy," Ralph said. "May I please see your search warrant?"

The G-men looked at each other. Kyle looked at Bert. The sheriff then said, "We really didn't think you'd ask....you've been cooperative before. Is one necessary?"

"You bet it is," Ralph said. "No search warrant, no lookie."

The four law officials stared at the three seated men for a moment. Then Bert said, "Bennie, we don't think you're involved in this whole thing. But if you know anything about the rocket you should now tell us."

Bennie said, "Bert, guys, I don't know anything about any rocket. Never heard of it."

Bert nodded and said, "Okay fellows. You need a warrant, we'll get a warrant." The four then turned and walked out the door.

After the law personnel had closed the door Bennie said, "Hey guys, is something going on here that I don't know about?"

Max said, "No Bennie. That sheriff just has it in for us for some reason. We don't know what he's talking about. Have you seen a rocket anywhere around here?"

Bennie thought, then said, "No, I haven't. But they sure seem to think we've got one."

Ralph and Max just shook their heads.

Outside the office building the four had gotten in their car and the sheriff was driving off. Just when he reached the main road he met the Kentucky Utilities truck coming in. Both vehicles stopped. The sheriff jumped out of his car and walked up to the KU truck. The driver rolled down the window and said, "Hey sheriff, I got a ladder to deliver here."

Bert said, "Yeah, we've been waiting for it. How about just unloading it here by the dirt road. We can't use it right now. We'll come back shortly and get it."

The driver said, "Anything you say. But I'm going to need help with it. It takes at least two very strong men to handle it. It weighs about 150 pounds."

"I'll help," Bert said. The two then opened the back truck doors. The driver reached in and slid the ladder partially out of the truck. He then said, "You grab the other end and we'll pull her out." They did, and then walked the ladder into the trees beside the BSC access road and dropped it.

Bert said with a grin, "It should be safe here unless two big strong bears come and carry it away."

The two then walked back to their vehicles, got in, and headed off the mountain.

Inside the sheriff's cruiser Bert said, "At least the ladder will be there when we get the search warrant and get back up here. It shouldn't take very long to rig it up to the column and verify that the rocket is inside. I'll call Judge Oakes right now to see if he'll have the warrant ready for us when we get back to Harlan."

The voice on the other end of the sheriff's cell phone said, "Good afternoon, Judge Oakes' chambers."

Bert said, "Hi Susan, this is sheriff Sterling. I need a favor and I need it fast. Could Judge Oakes sign a search warrant for us to go on the BSC property on Black Mountain?" He continued to give her all the particulars justifying the warrant.

Susan then replied, "Sheriff, I'll give this to the judge first thing in the morning. He's already left for the day. He was taking his wife to the Pine Mountain State Park in Pineville for dinner and a program there tonight. But he'll be back in chambers by 9 tomorrow morning. Will that be okay?"

Bert frowned and said, "Thanks Susan, I guess it'll have to be. I don't know how we could get a warrant before then. I'll be at your office tomorrow morning at 9.

I sure hope Judge Oakes can clear his docket of anything else scheduled until we get this warrant all taken care of."

"I'll see to it, sheriff," Susan said.

• • •

Later that day
BSC site
Black Mountain, Kentucky

Bennie had left the office at 5 o'clock. Ralph and Max had just locked up, got in their car, and started to drive to the Benham Hotel. When they got to the end of the BSC access road Ralph noticed the huge ladder lying in the leaves under some trees beside the road. He stopped the car and said, "Max, get out. We got some work to do."

Max and Ralph walked over to the ladder. Each got one end and they picked it up and started carrying it further back into the woods. Ralph insisted on their carrying it for about a half hour until they came to a cliff that was 70-80 feet high. They then pushed the ladder over the cliff. Ralph said, "If they were counting on using that ladder they better have a plan B."

They walked back to their car. It was now dark as they drove off Black Mountain.

• • •

At the same time
Harlan, Kentucky

The sheriff parked his cruiser at the Harlan County Court House. He turned off the motor, looked at the other three and said, "Unfortunately, that's going to be all we can do today. Let's meet at Judge Oakes' chambers tomorrow morning at 9. Hopefully we'll get that warrant and be on the road back to BSC shortly thereafter. I know tomorrow marks the beginning of the Thanksgiving holiday, but most folks will be working until the end of the work day. My guess is that for maximum impact from the bomb explosion whoever is behind this whole thing would want the most number of people on the road in their cars and in the air on planes. I have to think if that's the case the rocket would not be launched until late in the day. So I think we will have some time. Your thoughts?"

Agent King said, "That makes sense. But I really don't see we have any choice anyway. We've got to have the warrant or they won't let us back on the property. We just need to move it along as fast as we can."

Deputy Potter and Agent Short nodded agreement.

The four called it a day.

Chapter 25

Present Time
November 27
Harlan, Kentucky

"Sheriff, I just don't understand what has happened to Judge Oakes!" said his secretary, Susan. "He's always very punctual. As you are well aware, the judge is somewhat old fashioned and refuses to carry a cell phone. It's 9:30, let me call his home to see if I can find out anything from his wife."

"Appreciate it," said a worried sheriff. He was gathered in the judge's chambers in the Harlan County Court House, along with Deputy Potter and Agents Short and King. They had been there since 8:45.

"Okay, Mrs. Oakes, I appreciate it. You have a good day," Susan said into her phone. She then turned to the men and said, "Mrs. Oakes said the Judge left home at the usual time, about 8:40, and as far as she knew he was coming straight to the court house. Maybe he had an errand to run. I don't know any other way to make contact with him, do you?"

Bert shook his head and looked at his watch, "I guess we just wait."

Three hours later Judge Oakes walked into his chambers and said, "My, my what an impressive welcoming committee. I hope I didn't do something wrong!"

Susan said, "Judge, these gentlemen have been waiting for you since 8:45 this morning. We were afraid something bad had happened to you. Where have you been? Your wife said you left for work at the usual time."

The Judge got a worried look on his face and said, "Well, as we were getting back home from Pineville last night I noticed that the temperature gauge on my car indicated it was heating up. We got home okay and I forgot about it, but this morning as I was driving in I noticed again that it was overheating. Luckily I made it to Blanton's Auto Shop before it stopped. They had a few in front of me, so I've been waiting on my car over there all morning. I'm really sorry. And please, no lecture about carrying a cell phone!"

Bert said, "Judge, we are in a very, very serious situation and we need your immediate assistance. I think Susan has the paperwork all drawn up for a search warrant for the BSC site on Black Mountain. Every second is precious. I really don't have the time to go into all the details now, but just let me say that if we don't get up there asap thousands of people could be killed or injured. Please quickly look over the paperwork and sign so we can get going."

"I see," Judge Oakes said. He slid his glasses down over his nose and studied the paperwork a moment then took out his pen and signed the warrant.

"Thanks Judge," Bert exclaimed as he grabbed the warrant and then started running with Kyle and the 2 G-men to his cruiser. They jumped in and took off for Black Mountain.

About half way there Bert asked Kyle to call Rosie for him and put his phone on speaker so he could talk to her without taking his hands off the wheel. They were doing about 85 mph with their siren going.

"Hello. Sheriff's office, this is Rosie, how can I help you," came the voice over Bert's cell phone speaker.

"Hi Rosie," Bert said. "We finally got the search warrant, and are on our way to the BSC site. I really hate to ask you to do this, but you know how extremely important this Project BS is. I know we're coming up on the Thanksgiving holidays, but would you mind terribly to drive your cruiser up to the BSC site when you get off work? I'm thinking I might very well need your assistance with some of the paperwork and booking."

"Bert, that would not be a problem at all for me. But since the office will be closed a few days for Thanksgiving I'll have to bring Preacher Puss with me. She'll enjoy the outing, and will stay in the cruiser. Is that okay?"

"Super," the sheriff replied. We'll see you when you get there. I'll call you if there's any change. Drive carefully, you know that Black Mountain road is mighty curvy."

"Will do, chief," Rosie said. "See you sometime probably around 6:30." Rosie disconnected her phone.

Bert pressed the accelerator down a little more. The speedometer now registered 90 mph on the straight section of road.

• • •

Same time
BSC site
Black Mountain, Kentucky

Bennie, Ralph, and Max sat at their desks. Bennie said, "Well guys, it's almost 2 o'clock. Maybe Bert didn't have any luck getting a search warrant."

Ralph, whose desk sat in the middle, said, "I bet we see him soon." Max's desk sat to Ralph's left, and Bennie's to his right. The three desks sat in a row facing the entrance door. Just to the left of the door there was a full length mirror fastened to the wall.

Bennie was twirling the pencil in his hand when his face turned very pale. He dropped the pencil to the desk, and then picked it up and started to write on his desk note pad. He looked at the mirror and wrote the letters from Ralph's name plate affixed to the front of his desk. He wrote the letters: K E E L E N, as they appeared from the name plate in the mirror. He then turned to his left and said to Ralph, "You are Ralph Keelen. Neleek spelled backwards is Keelen. The sheriff was right, you boys are bad guys. I'm going to tell them when they get here."

Ralph slowly reached to his desk drawer and pulled it open. He pulled out a pistol, pointed it at Bennie's head, and said, "You'll not tell them anything, Bennie. Get your hands up and lets walk calmly over to the supply room. They did, and Max joined them. They opened the door to the supply room, grabbed a chair and shoved it into the room, and then told Bennie to sit in the chair. They then tied his hands and feet and put a cloth gag in his mouth.

Ralph spoke to Bennie, "We're going to close this door. If I hear one sound of any kind from you I'll start shooting through the door. Nod your head if you understand."

Bennie nodded. Ralph closed the door and spoke to Max, "Go out there and move Bennie's car over behind the storage building. Drive it into the woods as far as you can....just get it out of sight."

Bennie always left the keys in his car. Max went out and moved it as instructed, and then returned to the office building. He said, "Ralph, what will we tell the law when they get here? They'll miss Bennie."

"No problem," Ralph said. "We'll just say he wasn't feeling good and took the afternoon off."

Ralph continued, "Bennie was smarter than I gave him credit for. After all the time we've been here no one caught that my name was Keelen spelled backwards. But Bennie did. I really didn't want to hurt him. After we fire the rocket and leave they'll find him. He'll be okay."

Max smiled and said, "About 5 hours to go....it's looking better!"

Ralph said, "Max, they know who we are, and they know we've got the rocket here. Do you really think there's any chance we can launch it and then get away? I certainly can't follow my original plans. My identity is known. I'll probably now have to attempt to get out of the country and start a new life somewhere other than in the U.S.

Fortunately for us both, we were provided with fake id's and passports. I guess we just have to hope that we can pull things off here and then get to Atlanta and book a flight after things settle down. It's still possible, but I sure will feel better when we're off this mountain and headed for the airport."

Max replied, "Yeah....my thoughts pretty much as well. And it may well be a very long stay once we get to Atlanta. The airlines will be in chaos for days, if not weeks, after losing so many planes due to the nuclear blast. Fortunately, we've got plenty of money to get us through. But, first things first. We have to finish up here."

*   *   *

Same time

The sheriff's cruiser pulled into the BSC site. All the guys in the car were busy talking and failed to notice the absence of the ladder as they drove to the office building.

Ralph saw on the monitors the sheriff's car arriving. He said, "Okay Max, they're back. We just need to stay calm and get through this."

There was a banging on the door. Ralph shouted, "Come in."

The four entered. Sheriff Sterling walked to Ralph's desk and handed him the warrant.

Bert said, "That warrant gives us the right to search anywhere on your site, and we intend to do just that starting immediately."

Ralph looked at the sheriff and said, "It does appear to be just that. Please look around all you wish. We have nothing to hide."

Bert then said, "Where's Bennie?"

Max replied, "He wasn't feeling well, and took the afternoon off and went home."

Bert said, "Let's go get that ladder and carry it to the North West column. I think we'll find a rocket inside waiting to be discovered." The four turned and walked out of the office building and then down the dirt access road to where they had left the ladder.

"I was sure this was the spot where we left it," Bert said. He and the other three looked all around, but saw nothing.

Kyle said, "Bert, the leaves are disturbed here, and then going over in that direction. I think Ralph and Max got the ladder and carried it out of sight."

They all started following the trail of the disturbed leaves. After walking for almost a half hour they came to a cliff. Upon looking over it Bert pointed and said, "Well, we found it. For all the good it's going to do us now. Not only can we not drag it up this cliff, but it looks to be damaged beyond use."

The other three slowly shook their heads. Bert then pulled out his cell phone and dialed Kentucky Utilities. Agent Short pulled his cell phone and dialed Director Lester. They each told their situation, and then disconnected.

Ralph said, "The Kentucky Utilities dispatcher said the closest truck that had a long ladder was over in Bell County working a job. He said he'd do all he could to get it here asap."

Agent Short then said, "Director Lester seemed about to panic. He just told me he'd do what he could and hung up."

Bert looked at his watch. It was a little past 3 pm. He looked at the other three and said, "I think we just walk back and wait for the KU truck and ladder. I don't know anything else we can do, other than pray that rocket don't take off."

• • •

It started getting dark around 5 pm. At 5:45 headlights from a vehicle could be seen coming down the access road toward the office building. Ralph and Max were still inside. The sheriff, Deputy Potter, and the two G-men were standing outside beside their car.

"That's got to be it," Bert said. "We're in business!"

The big KU truck pulled up beside the sheriff's cruiser. The driver jumped out and said, "Hey Sheriff. I got here as soon as I could. My dispatcher called and said it was an extreme emergency. She said you called her first, and then right after your call she got one from the White House saying this was a national emergency and to get this ladder to you pronto. So here it is. It's sure not every day we get calls from the White House. What can I do?"

Bert replied, "Let's get it unloaded, and maybe you could help us carry it over to that far concrete column." Bert pointed toward the North West column.

"Glad to," the driver said. "Incidentally, my name's James Clark. Glad to be of service."

The ladder was moved to the column, leaned against it, and extended until it rested over the top rim.

James Clark then said, "If you intend for someone to climb up this ladder, I'll volunteer. I do it every day. I wouldn't want to see any of you get hurt."

Bert thought a moment and replied, "Sure, we'd appreciate that. But I have to tell you what you're looking for. We suspect there's a rocket inside that column. I see you have a flashlight on your belt. When you get to the top if you'd just lean over and look directly down into the column. We know it's hollow. We think when you shine your flashlight down there you'll see the pointed tip of the rocket. That's all we need to know. If it's there we can then arrest the people here responsible for it. Do you understand?

James Clark replied, "Shazamm. A rocket!! In Harlan County!! Yeah, I understand. Just climb up there and look into the column and see if I can confirm there's a rocket in there. I'll do it....and I can't wait to tell my friends about this one!" He started climbing.

Those standing at the base of the ladder watched Mr. Clark as he climbed up the 30 feet. He then reached down and retrieved his flashlight. He pointed it down into the column and turned it on. He then shouted, "Hey sheriff.....there's a rocket in here."

"Great!" shouted the sheriff. "That's all we needed to know. Come on back down and we'll get your ladder all loaded up."

Bert turned to the G-men and said, "How about you two go arrest Keelen and Baker. Kyle and I will help Mr. Clark get his ladder loaded."

"That won't be necessary, sheriff," Ralph Keelen shouted.

All looked toward the office building and saw Keelen and Baker walking toward them with guns pointed. "All of you slowly put your weapons on the ground, and then raise your hands above your head," Max shouted. They complied.

Ralph grinned and said, "It's about 6:20. In case you're interested that rocket will light up at exactly 7 pm. We're all going to have a really good view from here. Sit down and keep your hands up and behind your heads. We're just going to be quiet and wait until 7 pm. One move from any of you and we start shooting."

Chapter 26

Present Time

November 27

Harlan, Kentucky

osie looked at the clock. It was 5:20 pm. She
was running late. She grabbed her briefcase in
one hand and Preacher Puss in the other. She had
set the entrance door to lock when she left. She pushed
the door open with her foot, walked outside, and headed
for her cruiser. She got in and placed her briefcase and
Preacher Puss in the passenger seat. She said, "Preacher
Puss, we're running a tad late. I want you to be a good
kitty. Just sit there and watch all the pretty scenery as we
drive up to Black Mountain."

Preacher Puss swished her tail and purred. Rosie gave her a gentle pet.

When Rosie was almost to Cumberland she decided that she should give Bert a call just to report in and to tell him she was running a little behind. While stopped at a traffic light she dialed the sheriff's cell phone, put her phone on speaker, and set the phone in a cup holder. She heard the phone ring and ring and finally went to Bert's answering machine. He didn't answer. Rosie didn't think much about that. He could be busy. He always returns my calls promptly, she thought.

About 15 minutes later, around 6:30, she was passing through Benham and realized that Bert had not returned her call. She reached down and dialed his number again. Again the phone rang and rang without Bert answering. It finally went to his answering machine again. Rosie thought, Something is happening. It's very unusual for Bert to not either answer or return my calls. He could well have run into trouble with those BSC employees. They're known bad guys. I think when I get there I'd better approach the site very carefully.

• • •

Same time
White House Situation Room
Washington, D.C.

President DeVore, CIA Director Rudy Lester, Secretary of Defense Sam Back, and Homeland Security Secretary Josh Dillon all were gathered to monitor Project BS.

The president said, "Heck of a way to have to spend Thanksgiving Eve."

The other three nodded agreement. Director Lester said, "I just wish we knew exactly what's going on up on Black Mountain in Harlan County. I should have heard again from Cody Short by now. I'm getting nervous."

"You're always nervous, Rudy," President DeVore replied. "I got a good feeling about this whole thing. We've just got to hang in there. I feel certain we'll hear from them soon, and that the rocket has been neutralized."

Josh Dillon said, "Sure hope you're right, Mr. President. I've got a big turkey and a whole lot of family at home that I'd like to share Thanksgiving with tomorrow."

"Yeah, don't we all," Thomas DeVore said.

• • •

15 minutes later

Black Mountain

Harlan County, Kentucky

Rosie glanced at the clock on the dash board. It said 6:45. She was almost to the top of Black Mountain and still had not heard from Sheriff Sterling. She was worried.

She saw the BSC access road off to her left up ahead. She slowed and turned off her head lights. Fortunately, there was a full moon tonight, and it was already high in the sky. It provided enough light for her to slowly move down the access road. As she came to the clearing where the buildings and columns were located she was blocked by a Kentucky Utilities truck. She pulled up behind it and turned her motor off. She looked over at Preacher Puss and said, "Ole girl, we gotta be real quiet, and I'm going to slip out of the car and try and see what's going on."

She punched the button to open her car trunk, and then opened her door and got out. She didn't want to slam the door shut because that would make a loud noise, so she gently closed it....but it didn't completely close. She walked around to the trunk of her cruiser and pushed the trunk lid up and got her rifle out. She left the trunk open, not wanting to make noise by closing it. With her rifle pointed straight ahead she then moved around the KU truck toward the buildings. As soon as she got beyond the truck she could see the group gathered over by the columns. A light on a pole lit the area dimly. It looked like two men were holding pistols on five others that were sitting on the ground with hands up behind their heads. She recognized all of the sitting men except one, and she assumed he must be the KU truck driver. She slowly, slowly crept up behind the two men holding the guns. She noticed that one of them also was holding what looked to be some kind of a computer thing. It looked like a tablet computer. He had it in his left hand, and held a gun in his right.

Two things suddenly happened at the same time. (1) She felt something rubbing against her right ankle. She looked down and saw Preacher Puss looking up at her. The cat didn't object to rifles like she did to pistols. Rosie remembered she hadn't shut the cruiser door completely, and Preacher Puss had decided to accompany her. (2) There was suddenly a very loud roar. The area lit up like it was daytime for a brief few seconds, and the rocket shot out of the end of the concrete column headed straight up. It could be seen now only like a distant comet.

Suddenly the cat saw the pistol in Ralph's right hand. Almost as fast as the rocket she ran the short distance to him, leaped through the air with all four paws pointed toward his right arm....with claws extended. She landed with a thud on the middle of his lower right arm and the claws dug in deep. Ralph screamed in pain. He dropped his pistol, and then dropped the rocket control console from his left hand and tried to swat at Preacher Puss. By then the cat had noticed the gun in Max's hand and had jumped from Ralph to Max's right arm. Now it was Max's time to scream as her claws dug in. He dropped his gun and tried to shake the cat free. In doing so Preacher Puss was tossed into the air. When she came down she landed atop the rocket control console which had a blinking yellow light. Her right paw landed precisely atop the red button. When it did the yellow light stopped blinking. And there was silence.

"Get your hands up," Rosie shouted as she pointed the rifle toward Ralph and Max. The other five guys jumped to their feet. Ralph reached down to try and grab his pistol, but Kyle hit him in the stomach with his head as he made a leaping dive. The two fell together to the ground. Kyle delivered two well placed punches to Ralph's face, and Geek lost consciousness. Max started to run, but stopped quickly when Rosie fired two rounds beside his feet. He put his hands in the air. Sheriff Sterling walked over to him, jerked his arms down and behind his back, and placed cuffs on him. Kyle cuffed Keelen then slapped his face to wake him. He then stood him next to Max.

Agent Cody Short had his cell phone to his ear talking with Director Lester. Agent Sammy King started dancing around in circles, shouting, "We did it. We did it. We did it."

Bert looked down at Preacher Puss. She was standing beside Rosie, looking up at her, swishing her tail and meowing. Rosie laid her rifle on the ground and reached down and picked up the cat. Rosie petted her, and said, "Preacher Puss, you did it again. Your aim and your timing could not have been better. You are one remarkable cat!"

Bert said, "If I hadn't seen it with my own eyes I wouldn't have believed it. That cat just saved thousands of people from being killed, and prevented many, many more from being injured." He walked over and gave Preacher Puss a big kiss on the top of her head. The cat purred loudly.

James Clark had a very puzzled look on his face. He said, "I'm really not sure what I just saw. I know I saw it, but I still have a hard time believing it. I think something really good just happened, and do I ever have a story to tell my grandchildren!"

The sheriff said, "Okay lady and gentlemen, Project BS has now ended. The bomb didn't explode, and we caught the bad guys. Let's get everything all cleaned up here and head home for a wonderful Thanksgiving. Do we ever have something for which to be thankful!"

"Kyle, you, Rosie, and Preacher Puss take these two bad guys back to jail in your cruiser. I'll help James Clark load his ladder back up, and then the G-men and I will head for Harlan. We'll meet you at the office."

Kyle, Rosie, Preacher Puss, Ralph, and Max all loaded into Rosie's cruiser. She turned it around and they started the trip back down the mountain.

With two men on each end of the ladder, Bert, Cody, Sammy, and James Clark carried it to the KU truck and loaded it. James Clark then said, "Guys, I've been called on some strange calls during my career with Kentucky Utilities, but I can assure you this one takes the cake. I'm just glad I could be a part of Project BS.....whatever that is!!" He then laughed and shook hands with Bert and the two agents. He got in his truck, turned it around, waved good-bye and headed down the mountain.

Bert then said to the G-men, "Guys, let me just step in the office to make sure nothing's left there and to turn off the lights."

When he opened the office door he heard a thumping sound. He looked around and decided it was coming from the supply room. He walked over and opened its door.

There sat Bennie all tied up, gagged, and red-faced. Bert laughed, pulled the gag out, and started to untie him. Bert said, "Bennie, I'm sure glad you didn't get left. It was a good thing you could kick the door."

"Yeah," Bennie replied. "They tied my feet but didn't tie them to the chair. I could still swing em. I am so glad you heard me. And you sure were right, Ralph and Max are definitely bad guys."

Bert said, "They sure are. But we arrested them, and they're on their way to jail. Are you okay?"

"I'm fine, sheriff, thanks to you!"

"Okay, lets lock up here and then go look for your car. I bet they hid it in the woods out back."

Bert told the two Agents about Bennie, and then the four of them started looking behind the storage building for Bennie's car. They soon found it. Bennie drove it back to the access road. He then rolled down his window and shouted, "You guys have a super Thanksgiving. I'll see you in Harlan." The three waved to Bennie as he drove off.

Bert, Cody, and Sammy got in Bert's cruiser. As he started the engine he said, "They say all's well that ends well. This certainly has ended well. Let's get off this mountain and start a Thanksgiving with real meaning!"

Chapter 27

A few minutes earlier
White House Situation Room
Washington, D.C.

Director Lester held the cell phone to his ear. Suddenly his face lit up with a huge smile. He put the phone down and said, "Gentlemen, that was Agent Short calling from Black Mountain. He tells me the rocket did fire at precisely 7 pm, but that through some strange incident involving a cat, if I heard him correctly, the bomb explosion was aborted. And they have arrested both Keelen and Baker. Project BS is over. Happy Thanksgiving!"

President DeVore jumped up from his seat, spilling his soda on the conference table. He shouted, "Thank the good Lord. Thank the good Lord. Our prayers are answered." He then began dancing around the Situation Room.

Sam Back leaned over the conference table and lowered his head onto it. Tears of joy streamed down his face.

Josh Dillon gave a big thumbs up with both hands, and then got up and joined the President dancing around the room.

• • •

Same time
Pyongyang, North Korea

7:15 pm eastern standard time in the U.S. on Thanksgiving Eve corresponded to 8:15 am on Thanksgiving day in Pyongyang. Chairman Kim Jong-un sat very grim faced watching news broadcasts on several television monitors lining one wall in his office. He had just polished off a huge McDonald's breakfast, topped off with an extra half dozen pancakes. He knew that by now the news about his nuclear blast should be breaking on all the news networks. It wasn't. He thought, I'll give it another 30 minutes, then ask for General Ri to join me.

Ten minutes earlier General Ri got in his private car and started driving from Pyongyang to Shenyang, China.

His sources had told him of Project Bee Sting's failure. Being a prudent person, General Ri had already made plans in case of failure. He knew what his fate would be if he stayed in North Korea. He planned to drive north to the border town of Dandong, and to there cross over into China. It was then a short drive to Shenyang. He had several friends living there that would welcome him.

Chairman Kim looked at his watch. It was 8:45 am, and still nothing about the nuclear explosion on the news. He thought, It has failed. He punched the intercom button on his desk and said, "Send in General Ri."

After about 5 minutes his secretary spoke back through the intercom, "Chairman Kim, General Ri cannot be located."

Kim slammed his fist down so hard on his desk that his McDonald's coffee spilled onto his lap. His face turned beet red! His blood pressure sky rocketed!

• • •

Two hours later
Harlan, Kentucky

The two prisoners had been locked in the small holding cell in back of Sheriff Sterling's office. The sheriff now sat at his desk with Deputy Potter, Rosie Cain, and the two G-men seated in front of him. Bert said, "What a wonderful day we've had. I was really beginning to wonder there for a while if we were going to be successful, but it did all come together, Project BS is concluded with no deaths or injuries, and the bad guys are locked up. Couldn't ask for more than that."

Rosie had Preacher Puss in her lap. The cat had both eyes closed, was swishing her tail slowly, and purring. Rosie said, "How about this cat? She deserves a national medal of honor!"

"She does indeed," Bert replied. "But it'd be hard for her to wear. I guess she'll just have to be content with extra portions of Whisker Lickins."

All laughed. Agent Short then said, "Director Lester gave the good news to the President and his boys. They were just overjoyed. They said to thank each of you so very much, and to wish you a great Thanksgiving."

Agent Sammy King then said, "Cody and I are headed back to Washington, and likely won't see you good folks again. Before we leave I want to express our deepest gratitude for everything you did to bring Project BS to a successful conclusion."

Both Agents then stood up and walked over to Rosie and Preacher Puss. They each reached down and gave the cat a gentle stroke. Preacher Puss purred loudly in response. Agent King then said, "When we first arrived here Cody and I thought having that cat as a mascot in the sheriff's office was really some joke. Boy, were we wrong! How an animal could have her instincts is certainly beyond me. I just wish we could clone her and have a Preacher Puss clone in every law enforcement office!"

Bert then said, "It's been a long day. I know we're all very tired. I certainly want to thank each of you for your excellent service. I do hope you have a super Thanksgiving. I think we'll all rest well tonight."

• • •

Monday Morning
December 2
Harlan, Kentucky

Deputy Kyle Potter, Sheriff J. Bert Sterling, and Mayor Knapp were gathered at a back table in Creech Cafe. Each had a coffee cup sitting in front of them.

Mayor Knapp said, "I've heard the Thanksgiving Eve story now a couple of times, and I still find it hard to believe! We apparently came within seconds of actually having a nuclear bomb explode above Harlan County. Wow!"

Kyle said, "It was about as close as it could have been. That blinking light on the rocket control console apparently starts to blink just 5 seconds before the bomb is detonated. And it was blinking when Preacher Puss stepped on the red abort button. We were somewhere less than 5 seconds from the nuclear blast."

"Boy, unbelievable," Fred remarked.

The mayor then said, "What's going to happen to Keelen and Baker?"

Bert said, "Nothing good, I'm sure. I'm going to turn them over to the feds later today, and they'll pursue prosecution. They could be charged with a long stream of crimes. My guess is that they'll wind up in a federal prison somewhere, and likely grow old there."

"Hard to feel sorry for them," Fred said. "When you think, had that bomb exploded many, many people would have been killed or injured."

Fred then asked, "Did you hear who was behind the whole thing?"

The sheriff said, "Not really. But we have a strong suspicion. The two G-men told us the story about how Keelen had a friend at Wallops Island that turned out to be a North Korean mole. And that friend played a major part in Keelen's stealing the Aerobee rocket. That plus the fact that an apparently Russian submarine was involved in getting the nuclear warhead to the U.S. would certainly lead us to think that North Korea was likely behind everything. But we'll never know for sure."

Fred then said, "I'll tell you one thing, that rocket will likely find its way into a Harlan museum sometime in the future."

Bert laughed and said, "I wouldn't be surprised. It was sure strange how it landed in that farmer's pond. I understand he immediately called 911 and reported that he'd been attacked. I think he told the dispatcher that a huge rocket was stuck standing up in his pond. All kinds of federal and state officials then descended on the poor guy's farm to safely remove the rocket. I'm not sure where they took it, but Fred, you're right....one of these days it could return to Harlan to go into a museum. But that would be well off in the future. For the time being the government wants the fact that a nuclear bomb was actually launched from Black Mountain kept secret. And that's the reason there will be no press releases or news about Project BS. I'm sure that stories will leak out about the whole thing, but the general public won't be aware of the real threat for many, many years to come."

Kyle and Fred both nodded. Fred then said, "Well, on a brighter note, I've got some big news for you fellows!"

Bert and Kyle looked expectantly at the mayor, who then said, "I ran into Bennie Sekao at church yesterday. And that was yet another miracle related to this whole thing. After church I grabbed Bennie and the two of us had a good conversation about his excellent record while working for BSC, how he had completely changed his life around, etc. He then dropped his head and said he was worried now that he didn't have the job. I immediately told him that I wanted to hire him as my assistant manager here at Creech Cafe. Boy, did his eyes light up. He was so happy he started to jump up and down. I really needed a little help here anyway, so I just thought that hiring Bennie would be the thing to do. Of course he readily accepted, but did say he would like a couple of days off to recuperate from the BSC thing. I told him to take all the time required. I think he's going to start on Wednesday. How about that!"

The sheriff and the deputy both beamed at Fred. Bert said, "Fred, you really are a good egg. I'm so happy for Bennie, and I do think he'll make you an excellent employee. Just don't start serving any alcoholic beverages!"

Fred laughed, "Don't worry ....that'll never happen."

Bert then said, "Thanks for everything, Fred. Kyle and I gotta get going. I think I'm going to drive to

Maggard's Grocery and explain to Trigger Green how everything turned out. He tried his best to be helpful, and did share what he knew about Keelen, or Neleek as he was then known. But before Kyle and I get back on the job, how about a story to start the week off?"

Fred smiled and started, "The weekend edition of the Harlan Daily Enterprise carried a good one. This fellow had recently gotten a new primary care physician. After a couple of visits and many lab tests the doc told the fellow that he was doing pretty well for his age. Somewhat concerned about that comment, the fellow asked, 'Doc, do you think I'll live to be 80?' The doctor then asked the fellow if he smoked or drank beer or wine. 'Oh no,' he replied, 'I don't do drugs either.' The doctor then asked, 'Do you eat steak or barbecued ribs?' He replied, 'Oh no, my previous doctor told me all red meat is bad for you.' The doctor said, 'Do you spend a lot of time in the sun, doing things like playing golf, sailing, hiking, or bicycling?' 'Sure don't,' the fellow replied. 'Do you gamble, drive fast cars, or have a lot of sex?' the doctor asked. 'I don't do any of those things,' replied the fellow. The doctor then looked at the fellow and said, 'Then why do you want to live to be 80?'"

Kyle stood and slapped Fred on the back. Bert laughed and said, "I think we're off this week to a good start....thanks Fred."   The two lawmen walked out of Creech Cafe.

• • •

One hour later
Maggard's Grocery
Wallins, Kentucky

Bert walked into the store and looked over to the check-out counter. Fatso looked at him and grinned. "Hey sheriff, good to see you. What can I do for you?"

"Just here to chat with Trigger for a few minutes if he's available."

"Yeah, he's back there. But before I press the button to unlock his door you've got to tell me why elephants don't use computers?"

Bert thought a moment and said, "Fatso, I just really don't know!"

Fatso said with a chuckle, "Because they're afraid to use the mouse!"

"Press the button."

The sheriff walked back to Trigger's door and knocked. The voice on the other side said, "Come in, come in."

The two shook hands and seated themselves. Trigger said, "Bert, I've heard from the grapevine that there was some serious stuff that took place over the weekend on Black Mountain. Can you share any of it with me?"

Bert grinned and said, "You read my mind, Trigger. That's the purpose of my visit. I knew you were interested in helping us find that rocket, so I wanted to give you the update."

Trigger replied, "Thanks, Bert. I would appreciate hearing it."

The sheriff then told Trigger most of the details about the weekend happenings at the BSC site. He left out anything he felt was confidential.

Trigger then leaned back in his chair and said, "Well, well, well. I sure am glad to hear that. I was honestly worried to death about all the problems that rocket could cause us. It sounds like everything certainly got taken care of in good fashion. But I'll tell you one thing, the role that Preacher Puss had is hard to swallow. But that cat has done some mighty remarkable things in the past, so I'll certainly take your word for it. Tell Rosie to give her extra Whisker Lickins!"

Bert laughed, stood, and said, "That I will do, my friend. Thanks for your help and concern. Take care."

As Bert was walking toward the grocery store's entrance door Fatso saw him and shouted, "Hey Bert, how do you stop an elephant from smelling?"

Bert continued walking.

"You tie a knot in his trunk!" shouted Fatso with a laugh.

As he started through the door Bert yelled, "You have a good day, Fatso."

• • •

One hour later
Harlan, Kentucky

Bert was leaning on the counter talking to Rosie, "I hope you, Preacher Puss, and your family had a great Thanksgiving."

Rosie replied, "We sure did. After all that excitement and activity on Black Mountain we were ready for a nice peaceful holiday. It was delightful, wasn't it Preacher Puss?"

The cat, lying on her shelf beside the entrance door, had one eye slightly open as she put forth a meow.

Just then the door opened and Pastor Raymond Bell entered the office. "Greetings, greetings one and all," he said, and then walked over to Bert, shook hands, and then leaned across the counter and gave Rosie a big hug.

Bert said, "That was a mighty good sermon yesterday, Raymond."

"Glad to hear it was meaningful to you, sheriff," replied the pastor. "I just wanted to stop by to tell you guys that the congregation had been praying mightily for a good resolution on the unknown problem for which you asked prayer. And then I heard a few rumors over the weekend about strange things going on. So I just thought I'd check to see if you could share anything with me."

"Glad to," Bert replied. "I think those prayers were indeed answered. We were able to avert a major tragedy that could well have killed and injured thousands. And the very strange way things were resolved just had to have been guided from Him above through that cat lying over there."

All three turned to look at Preacher Puss. She then opened both eyes, stood up, swished her tail, and meowed loudly.

Pastor Bell walked over beside her and said, "Well, the Lord does work in mysterious ways." He then reached up to Preacher Puss and held out the palm of his right hand. Preacher Puss raised her right paw and 'high fived' the pastor.

As Pastor Bell walked out, Bert said, "The Lord does indeed work in mysterious ways!"

www.ingramcontent.com/pod-product-compliance
Lightning Source LLC
Chambersburg PA
CBHW050858130726
47900CB00013B/342